A SHOT OF SCANDAL

A CAFE CRIMES COZY MYSTERY

SIMONE STIER

A Shot of Scandal
A Cafe Crimes Cozy Mystery

Simone Stier

© 2024 Simone Stier
All Rights Reserved

This book may not be reproduced without the written consent of the publisher. Except for review quotes.

This is a work of fiction. All people, places, names, and events are products of the author's imagination or a mysterious coincidence.

❦ Created with Vellum

To amateur sleuths everywhere ...

PROLOGUE

The night of the Beauregard gala, two things happened in the small town of Magnolia Grove.

First: a robbery.

Second: a murder.

But before we dive into that piping-hot mess, let me introduce myself. I'm Parker Hayes, and if there's one thing I've learned from my podcasting days, it's that you can't brew a good story without first grinding the beans.

Picture this ... Magnolia Grove, a charming Southern town where sweet tea flows like water and gossip spreads faster than butter on a hot biscuit. Enter yours truly, a former true-crime podcaster trying to reinvent herself as a cafe owner. Throw in a cast of colorful characters, each with their own secret recipe for trouble, and you've got yourself a right fine setup.

Oh, and did I mention the murder? Yeah, we'll get to that. But first, let me pour you a cup of my signature blend and tell you how I, Parker Hayes, went from serving up true-crime stories to serving lattes in a town where the secrets are as rich as my espresso. Trust me, this tale is best savored slowly, just like a good cup of joe.

Now, where should I begin? Ah yes, the day after I rolled into Magnolia Grove with nothing but three suitcases and a dream ...

CHAPTER 1

In the heart of the charming storybook town of Magnolia Grove, the square buzzed with activity, the air was alive with the chatter of locals and the rustle of shopping bags. The scent of fresh-cut grass drifted in the warm breeze as I strolled through town. Hope and determination fueled my steps. After all, I was starting a new chapter in my life. Just the previous day, the Greyhound had unceremoniously dropped me and my three bags at the edge of town, the bus's exhaust was a final farewell to my old life.

I recently hung up my microphone as the host for my popular podcast *Criminally Yours, Your Daily Shot of Murder*, and left the big city to relocate to the slower pace of Magnolia Grove, North Carolina. Just a blip on the map nestled near the foothills of the Blue Ridge Mountains, where crime was non-existent, and the tree-lined streets radiated with charm. Their motto: "Where Our People Are as Sweet as Our Blossoms." I poured my life savings into a worn-down corner store located in a historical building once known as Elliot's Drugs, a bustling pharmacy and soda fountain back in the day, to fulfill my dream of opening a coffee and dessert cafe, Catch You Latte. My reason for taking such a huge leap of faith? Peace of mind. I wanted to shift gears from the fast lane into a slow mosey. My big plan was to sell specialized coffees and scrumptious desserts to the community. According to my research, what was lacking from Magnolia Grove was a neighborhood cafe. And the closest thing to passable coffee was the Dunkin' Donuts in the next town over. Despite the enormous decision to uproot my life and plunder my savings account, I couldn't wait to get started renovating the location for my future cafe.

I'd been dreaming of a fresh start for several years. The wear and tear of doing the podcast and living in the big city had finally taken its toll, and my nerves were shot. As I said, I longed for a simpler life where I could brew coffee, serve yummy desserts and pastries and have light-hearted conversations with regular folks that didn't involve, well, crime. I pictured my shop as an inviting haven where locals could meet up and share quality time together. I could see myself in the early morning hours, mixing ingredients for my easy-to-bake, yet tasty treats—blueberry muffins, my grandmother's famous cinnamon rolls, and of course my favorite, chocolate chip cookies. I could already smell the enticing aromas of sugary sweets filling the place, coupled with the aroma of my favorite coffee blends. And after the last customer strolled off to do whatever it was people did in Magnolia Grove, I'd commute to my cozy and welcoming apartment right upstairs, above the shop. That was my plan, anyway.

These thoughts lifted my weary soul as I walked through town. But as I approached the vacant building, I felt a pang of fear and doubt. The crumbling facade and cracked windows evidenced years of abandonment.

"Uh-oh."

Suddenly this project of whipping the building back into shape appeared colossal and daunting, if not impossible.

Think positive, Parker. Look beyond the decay and glimpse the possibilities.

Yes, it would take serious hard work, but it would be worth it in the end. That's what I hoped, anyway.

I crossed the street and headed to the entrance, where an older man stood waiting in front of the chain-locked door. He wore baggy jeans, a faded tee and a raggedy baseball cap that looked like it had been around for quite some time. His puffy white beard was a bit unkempt and gave him a slight resemblance to Santa. He seemed like the kind of man who could hug you and remind you that everything would be okay. He smelled like fresh soap and sawdust. I liked him immediately.

"You must be Parker Hayes." He extended his hand and widened his smile. "Clyde Honeycutt, your handyman extraordinaire."

I reached out and put forth a hearty shake. "Nice to meet you, Mr. Honeycutt."

"Aw, you can call me Clyde, sweetie. No pretense here."

"Well, nice to meet you, Clyde." I looked at the neglected building. "Looks like we've got our work cut out for us."

He tipped back his cap, gazed up at the building and whistled. "She's a beauty, though. Well, she was in her heyday."

I dug around in my bag and pulled out a key for the chain lock. "I'm excited to see the inside and start working on a plan of attack."

I slipped the key into the lock, and Clyde helped me unwrap the clanking metal chain. When I couldn't get the door to budge, he used the better half of his weight to force the wooden door open with a loud crack. I winced as some of the wood splintered and fell to the ground.

"It's fixable," Clyde said, kicking a large piece of the splintered wood to the side.

I would come to know the words "it's fixable" were Clyde Honeycutt's mantra.

Inside the abandoned shop, the first thing that hit me was the decades of mustiness and mildew. The dank air was thick and permeated the place. It didn't help that my sense of smell was borderline superhuman. A blessing and a curse. I kept the door propped open in hopes of letting some of the stale air escape.

Clyde removed a flashlight from his pocket and searched the wall for a light switch. When he flicked the switch a few times and nothing happened, he took out another flashlight from his pocket and handed it to me. Another thing I would come to know was that Clyde Honeycutt was a walking toolbox.

I aimed the beam of light through the darkness. "I notified the utility company and paid them, but I guess something must be broken."

Clyde chuckled. "I reckon a lot of things are broken."

I felt the weight of despair fill my chest. "It's pretty bad, huh? It didn't look this messed up in the pictures online."

That got Clyde rolling with laughter. "That sounds about right." When Clyde detected my sinking hope, he said, "Aw, don't let it get you down, sweetie. It's fixable."

I was grateful for Clyde's faith in fixing things because in that moment mine was waning. But he seemed to know what he was talking about. My "expertise" in these matters came solely from home renovation TV shows. They made it look so easy to just knock down a few walls, redo the floors, add some built-ins and new fixtures, then decorate with some eclectic pieces of furniture and doodads and voila... perfection.

As I surveyed the dilapidated space, my phone buzzed in my pocket. Mom's smiling face lit up the screen. I stepped outside to take the call.

"Hi, Mom," I answered, trying to inject some enthusiasm into my voice.

"Parker, honey! How's the big move going? Your father and I are so excited for you!"

I sighed, looking back at the run-down building. "It's... going. The place needs a lot more work than I expected."

"Oh, honey, remember when you were little, and I'd create those challenging puzzles for you? You'd sit there for hours, determined to solve them. This is just another puzzle, and I know you'll figure it out."

I remembered those quiet afternoons spent at our kitchen table, the scraps of Mom's latest quilt project scattered about and the scent of animal dander from Dad's veterinary scrubs. They had always supported my penchant for problem-solving, nurturing it in ways that led me to where I am today.

"Thanks, Mom. I needed that reminder."

"Hold on, your father wants to say hello."

There was a brief shuffling sound before the top half of Dad's head appeared on the screen. "Hey there, Sherlock! How's my favorite pod-show host doing?"

I chuckled. "It's *podcast*, Dad. And I'm not doing that anymore, remember? Can you move the phone down so I can see your *whole* face?"

"Right, right. Well, how's my favorite ex-pod-show host doing then? Solved any local mysteries yet? Found out who stole the town's last can of coffee, perhaps?"

"Dad," I groaned, but I was smiling. "I'm okay, just feeling a bit overwhelmed."

"Well, kiddo, you know what they say—when life gives you lemons, make lemonade. And if you can't make lemonade, well, at least you've got some lemons for those scones you love to make!"

I shook my head but felt lighter. "I'll keep that in mind."

"Listen, Parker, you've got the sharpest mind I know. Whether it's solving puzzles, making a pod-show, sniffing out crimes—literally and figuratively. Hahaha ... You'll be just fine renovating that building. The key is patience and persistence. You've got this, Sherlock."

"Thanks, Dad."

After exchanging a few more words and promising to call soon, I hung up. As I stared at my phone, I thought about the last time my parents had visited me in the city. The mugging had shaken us all and deterred them from ever visiting again. It was one of the reasons I'd decided to move to Magnolia Grove—a place where they might feel safe enough to visit me once more.

I inhaled, squared my shoulders and headed back inside. Mom was right: this was just another puzzle to solve. And solve it I would, one piece at a time.

"Everything hunky-dory?" Clyde asked as I re-entered.

"Yeah." I felt a renewed sense of determination. "Just got a pep talk from my mom and dad. Now, where were we?"

Clyde looked past me and grinned. "We're fixing to have a tornado."

I was about to ask what he meant when in swept a woman wearing a flower-patterned tunic, which was billowing around her as if she'd ridden in on a gust of wind. She flipped her long cascade of honey-blonde waves over her shoulder.

"Heavens to Betsy!" she exclaimed, her voice filling the dusty space. The scent of sticky sweet gardenias drifted through the musty room.

"Morning, Nellie," Clyde pointed to me. "This is Miss Parker Hayes, Magnolia Grove's newest resident."

Nellie sashayed over, offering a butterfly of a handshake. "Pleasure to meet you. I'm Nellie Pritchett, the head of Magnolia Grove's welcoming committee. My official job is town clerk. I advise the mayor and town council on all matters."

I could see that Nellie was a force of nature in her own right. "Nice to meet you."

Clyde nudged me. "She also knows where all the bodies are buried."

"Well, I do have access to all the old documents and records, Clyde." While her sparkling eyes reflected joy and optimism, beneath the surface I detected a hint of something shrewd about her. I concluded that Nellie Pritchett was the town's official busybody.

Nellie swept her long hair over her shoulder again and retrieved a flyer from her oversized and jam-packed tote bag. "I just came by to say welcome. If you ever need anything with records or permits, come see me. I'll get you squared away in no time flat."

"Thanks. I'll do that."

"Oh yes, and I want to extend an invitation to the gala being held at the Beauregard mansion this evening."

I took the flyer with some reluctance. I wasn't prepared for a gala, not only because of my gala-free wardrobe. I really wanted to focus on the cafe. This was evidently shaping up to be an around-the-clock project for me.

Nellie continued twittering away. "It's the event of the season! The Magnolia Rose necklace will be on display for the first time in decades. Along with other family heirlooms. The Beauregards have graciously invited everyone in town to partake."

I exhaled and motioned around me. "I'd love to go, but I

think I'll be burning the midnight oil trying to figure out how to tackle this beast of a project."

Nellie waved the air. "Nonsense! Work can wait. Trust me, Miss Hayes, you don't want to miss it. Doing so would be an unfortunate mistake."

Yikes. I wasn't sure what that meant, but Nellie sure knew how to apply the pressure.

I quickly thought of another out. "Oh, um ... Unfortunately, I don't have any gala-appropriate clothing with me."

Nellie let out a soft chuckle and fluttered her hand about. She was not one to be deterred. "Just stop by Maggie's. She'll get you all fixed up. It's a hop, skip, and a jump away. Walk out your front door, go right past the jewelry shop, Sparkle & Shine, then pass the flower shop, Blossom and Bloom. Cross the street towards Henderson's Hardware—Maggie's shop, Boutique Chic on Main, is right down the block on the corner."

Nellie could navigate the town's shops blindfolded. I looked to Clyde for some backup, but my handyman moved away from the conversation to measure the location where the new counter would go at the back of the shop.

Finally, I threw out my last-ditch effort. "I appreciate the invite, but to be honest, I prefer not to go alone." I hoped this last excuse would get the busy-body Nellie Pritchett off my back.

It didn't.

"Nonsense. Clyde, honey, why don't you swing by the Garden Inn—I'm assuming that's where you're staying,

Parker, since it's the only decent place in town—and pick up Miss Hayes on your way this evening."

Part of me was grateful to have this complete stranger inviting me to a social gathering on only my second night in town. The other part of me felt unprepared to hobnob at a gala event. I had planned to ease my way into the community, not be thrown into the deep end.

"Sure thing. I'll pick you up, Parker," Clyde said.

I shot him a glance. He winked back and continued measuring. The double-crosser.

Nellie clapped and gave me a sugary beam. "It's settled then. We'll see you tonight! I'll make certain you receive a warm welcome. I know you'll come to love the folks of Magnolia Grove in a very special way."

As she swooped out of the shop, I thought her parting words sounded a bit odd. A very special way?

Clyde ambled over, carrying a clipboard. "Why don't you go over yonder to Maggie's and get situated while I finish up in here."

Dress shopping was not on my agenda, nor was I in the mood for it. There was too much work to do!

"Shouldn't I stick around to help?"

He shook his head. "Not much to help with at this here juncture. I'm just getting a read on the place and gathering details."

"But that's my specialty. I love gathering details."

"Appreciate it, but I'm good. Now you get on down to Maggie's."

I gazed around the run-down space. The dinginess, dust and debris along with the scuffed floors was a vast contrast to my vision of a cozy and welcoming atmosphere. This was the backdrop of a horror movie.

Clyde tapped me with the clipboard. "Everything's going to be okay, Parker. We'll get this place fixed up faster than a Midwest tornado."

I grinned at the jovial handyman. "Honestly, Clyde, I don't like shopping. Or parties." I didn't go into my reasons—Clyde didn't need to know about my quirks.

"Try not to overthink it."

"What time is this thing?" I looked at the flyer.

"Starts at six o'clock. I'll drive. I'll be outside the Inn at quarter till."

~

THE PASTEL PINK siding storefront of Maggie's Boutique Chic on Main had a large, inviting bay window displaying dresses and gowns. Outside the entrance, cascades of flowers draped over the sidewalk sign, which announced a fifty-percent-off sale.

I entered the shop, and the citrusy fragrance of peonies tickled my nose and brought on a sneeze. I would definitely have to get used to all these overwhelming perfumes and scents. The racks of frilly and colorful dresses and crammed shelves of accessories added to the sensory overload.

Behind the counter stood presumably Maggie Thomas, a slender woman with wild red curls and a glamorous magazine-ready face. Her colorful patterned dress with its puffy sleeves screamed trendy. I quickly concluded that

Maggie was the town's authority on all things fashion and elegance. I also suspected her shop was the hub the social crowd frequented. One could undoubtedly find something for any occasion within this enchanting boutique.

She looked up from the counter, which was cluttered with papers and envelopes stamped "past due."

I approached.

Her eyes assessed me with curiosity. "Hello!" Maggie exclaimed in a sing-song voice. "You must be Parker Hayes, the woman who bought Elliot's Drugs."

Maggie's overzealous greeting, coupled with the fact she already knew about me, was both fascinating and mildly alarming. Information traveled at warp speed in Magnolia Grove.

"Yes, I am. Nice to meet you," I said.

"You sure got yourself into something with that one. It's been vacant for decades."

I tucked my hair behind my ear. "It will undoubtedly take some elbow grease."

Maggie let out a sultry laugh. "I'd say about ten tons worth! What brings you in today? Let me guess … you need something fabulous for the Beauregard gala tonight?"

"How'd you know?"

Maggie reapplied some gloss to her plump lips and came out from behind the counter. "This is a small town. Everybody knows everything about everyone. You'll get used to it. Come on, I'm sure I have just the thing! Something simple and refined, just like you."

I didn't consider myself refined. Simple, maybe, but more in a sporty and casual way. I leaned more toward low-key but presentable. But I could tell it would be impossible to rein in the likes of Maggie Thomas. Her face sparkled with palpable excitement as she led me toward a row of elegant gowns. I stood back a bit and watched the enthusiastic artistry with which she whipped through the selection.

"Let's see …" Maggie gazed over her shoulder and sized me up. "I'm sure I have just the thing!" she chirped again.

"I'm not exactly the gown-wearing type."

Maggie ignored me and continued flipping through the dresses. "Don't you worry about that! I'll get you all set up. This is my specialty."

"Sounds good. I guess. I mean … I'll leave it to you."

"So, have you met any of the Beauregards yet? They're an interesting bunch. Filthy rich. They own most of the town." Her tone had slipped from boisterous to a tad conspiratorial.

"Not yet. I just got here yesterday. But I'm sure by the end of this evening I'll have the entire backstory on everyone in town…"

"You just might. So, I heard you have a podcast about crimes. That's exciting. What's your biggest story? I love a good mystery!"

I forced a smile, careful not to reveal my weariness over a past I had moved on from. I certainly didn't want to share my innermost thoughts on this topic with Maggie Thomas. Sure, she seemed nice, but…

"I've closed that chapter in my life and have moved on. I'm looking forward to settling into my new crime-free existence here in Magnolia Grove. Fresh starts and all that. I'm excited about my cafe."

"Oh, aren't we all! I don't think this place even knows what a decent cup of coffee tastes like. You have a name for it yet?"

"It's going to be called Catch You Latte."

"Isn't that delightful!" Maggie continued shuffling through the dresses. "Well, you've certainly come to the right place for a slower pace. And don't worry, I won't pry into your business ... too much. Ahh ... here we go!"

She pulled out a violet gown from the rack and held it up against my chest.

"Oh, this is perfect. Such a great color for you. Brings out your eyes. And it'll look perfect with your dark shade of brown hair."

I looked at myself in the tall mirror and admired the scooped neckline. She was right, the color did suit me.

"This is beautiful, but do you think it will be ... over the top?" I took the dress and held it up against myself.

Maggie beamed with pride. "Everything about the Beauregards is over the top. It's perfect for the occasion. Trust me on this one."

Not having a clue what to expect at the gala, I had no choice but to trust Maggie Thomas. From what I'd gathered about the Beauregards in just a few minutes with her, it seemed safer to be overdressed than underdressed. After all, fitting in was crucial—no one wants to be a walking fashion faux pas on their second night in town.

I purchased the gown along with a pair of shoes and some simple yet sparkly earrings Maggie had picked out.

She gave me fifty percent off, plus a newcomer discount, which I appreciated. I had a decent chunk of change from selling my condo in the city along with royalties from the podcast, but those funds were dwindling. And based on the condition of the building I'd purchased, I would be broke in no time.

"Thank you, Maggie. I really appreciate your help."

"Don't you worry about a thing, darlin'. You're gonna knock 'em dead. See you tonight!"

CHAPTER 2

Outside of the Garden Inn, I stood under the awning and waited for Clyde to pick me up for the gala. The honey glow of the day's end filtered over the lush flower garden across the street. I had to say, Maggie's dress selection was transformative. I felt elegant, confident and well-prepared for an evening of awkward mingling and small talk.

Clyde pulled up in a vintage sports convertible and whistled. "Well, looky here. Parker Hayes."

My handyman cleaned up well in his seersucker suit, his gray hair slicked back. He'd even tamed his beard for the occasion.

Clyde kept the top down but drove at a mindful pace to avoid mussing my hair, which I had painstakingly pulled up into a twist with a few tendrils framing my face. The Beauregard estate was situated on sprawling grounds at the edge of Magnolia Grove. As the convertible approached the opulent mansion, I marveled at its stately columns and wraparound porches. The whole place glowed under the golden dusk. Elegant lanterns lined the driveway, guiding our path to the entrance, where valets in black uniforms awaited. We pulled up and Clyde tossed one of the men his keys. We got out and we walked up a red-carpeted staircase to the grand double doors.

Once inside, we meandered toward the ballroom and acknowledged a few of the other well-dressed guests. We entered the expansive ballroom, which shimmered under the soft illumination of the many crystal chandeliers. Ladies with sparkling jewelry glided over the gleaming marble floors. Men stood off on the sidelines chatting in small clusters. The aroma of savory appetizers drifted in the air as the waitstaff in their crisp uniforms carried trays and made pitstops, offering their delectable selections.

We stopped and stood in a less crowded space. One of the servers came by with a tray. Clyde reached for something that resembled a bite-size sandwich. He grabbed two of them and handed me one.

"Ever had North Carolina barbecue?" he asked.

"No, I'm more of a turkey sandwich girl myself."

"Well, you just try this. Pulled pork."

I bit into the small sandwich. The pulled pork melted in my mouth. "Oh, that's good," I said with my mouth full and already looking for another waiter to come by with more.

An older gentleman with a gray combover and a wiry frame slapped Clyde on the back. "Clyde Honeycutt, good to see you, old chum."

"Dr. Rufus Delacroix. Good to see you," Clyde said, gesturing to me. "I'd like to introduce you to Magnolia

Grove's newest resident, owner of Magnolia Grove's soon-to-be neighborhood cafe, Parker Hayes."

Rufus reached for my hand. "Pleasure to meet you, Parker."

"Nice to meet you too, Rufus," I said, shaking his hand.

"Rufus is a retired professor of archeology, specializing in historical artifacts."

"Oh, you make me sound old, Clyde. Well, I guess I am. Retirement just means I have more time to spend on my hobbies." He looked at his watch. "I'm thrilled to be here tonight. This gala is a treasure trove of stories and history. And that Magnolia Rose necklace is a beauty. Oh, to be able to hold the weight of those gems in my hands would be something. But unfortunately, I will only be able to behold it with my eyes, which is fine with me. There is quite some mythology behind that necklace." He looked at his watch again.

Clyde chuckled. "Rufus, I think you'd marry that thing if you could."

"Ha. Well, I've got to skedaddle. Duty calls."

"Okay, see ya, buddy," Clyde said.

Rufus gave me a polite nod, pressed down his combover and skittered off.

"Interesting fellow," I said, watching Rufus.

"He's a character."

Rufus meandered his way through the crowd and approached an elegant older woman with silver hair styled in an intricate updo. Her posture exuded authority, and her designer ivory gown sparkled under the chandeliers. Rufus Delacroix leaned in close, speaking in hushed tones. The woman's face tightened, her eyes narrowing as she listened. Their conversation seemed intense, laced with frantic gestures from the doctor and curt nods from the woman.

I turned to Clyde. "Clyde, who is that woman Dr. Delacroix is talking to? The one in the sparkling gown?"

Clyde followed my gaze to the pair. "Ah, that would be Evelyn Beauregard herself. The lady of the house and hostess of this fine affair. Formidable woman, that one."

After a moment, the two of them glanced around the room, as if checking to see if anyone was watching. Then, almost in unison, they slipped out of the main hall.

Clyde's attention had already gone elsewhere. "Hey, Trent Ashworth is waving me down."

I looked over to a man with a barrel chest holding an unlit cigar in his mouth.

"I'd introduce you, but trust me, you don't wanna meet him. He tells crude jokes and would probably make at least ten passes at you before the conversation was over."

I laughed and patted Clyde's shoulder. "No worries. If I'm feeling like I need some attention, I'll come over."

"I'll be right across the room if you need me. But I suspect you'll be fine on your own."

Clyde parted, and I decided to venture around the ballroom. I was greeted with cordial and curious smiles from the gathering of guests as they bantered together and popped appetizers into their mouths. A four-string quartet played in the background. I caught murmurs of subdued excitement as the guests waited for the parlor doors to open. Soon, the cherished Magnolia Rose necklace and other family heirlooms would be on display for all to see. I found myself starting to get caught up in the anticipation of seeing the famed necklace rumored to be worth a small fortune.

"Oh, Parker! You look stunning!" Maggie Thomas of Boutique Chic approached and gave an airy hug. She had on an orange-red gown that matched her wild hair. Her entire presence reminded me of a flame.

"Thanks to you!"

"Well, just doing my job." She gazed around the room. "See, what did I tell you? Filthy rich …"

"Sure seems like it. This is a lovely place."

Maggie looked over at the nearby grandfather clock. "Still another half hour until they open the parlor. Well, enjoy yourself, Parker."

After making another sweeping round of the vast ballroom and eating two more pulled pork sliders and what I found out was fried okra, I stationed myself under an enormous painting of a stately gentleman to do some people-watching.

Across the room, a handsome gentleman sporting a perfectly tailored khaki suit caught my attention. His dark hair highlighted a hint of silver at his temples. He noticed me noticing him, then sauntered over. The closer he got, the faster my heart raced. I felt a bit rusty when it came to handsome and alluring men.

"Good evening, I'm Whit Hawthorne."

Whit exuded a warm and inviting scent of vanilla with just a hint of lemon.

"Parker Hayes," I said, the flutter of excitement in my

chest growing stronger. I fought to keep my composure. "I'm new in town."

"Parker." His voice carried a smooth and measured drawl. "What a pleasure to meet you."

"Likewise."

"You're the one who bought the old drugstore."

I felt a flush of embarrassment wash over me. "Yes, I am. Did someone write an article about me or something?"

Whit gave me a flirty grin. "Ha. You'll get used to news traveling fast in a small town like this. Besides everyone knowing your business, how are you liking Magnolia Grove?"

"It's only my second night here, but so far, it's been pleasant. Everyone is so warm and welcoming."

He grinned. "And in my humble opinion, I'm guessing a bit nosy."

"I'm guessing just curious about the woman who was foolish enough to buy the most dilapidated building in town."

He raised his glass in a salute. "Foolish? Or brave? Maybe a bit of both."

"Let's go with brave."

Whit's deep brown eyes sparkled with amusement. "Bravery suits you. What are your plans for the place?"

"It's going to be an overhaul, but when it's finished sometime in the next century, it'll be a cafe that sells specialty coffees as well as simple desserts."

His smile didn't fade. "I'm not alone in my sentiments when I tell you we could use some good coffee around here. What are you going to call it?"

"Catch You Latte."

"Clever."

"So, what is it that you do, Whit?"

"I'm the town historian."

"Town historian? They still have those?" I cringed at my awkwardness.

Again, Whit smiled and brushed it off as though some bumbling puppy had just licked his cheek.

"I know, we're a dying breed, and I'll probably come looking for a job at Catch You Latte someday. But for now, yes, there are still a few of us in existence. And the beauty is, Magnolia Grove is steeped in rich history."

We both looked around at the ballroom teeming with extravagance.

I turned to Whit. "Definitely rich…"

"Mm hmm."

"Sounds like you'd be just the guy to talk to about the building I bought. For instance, why is it in such bad shape? Everything else around is so charming and well-kept."

Whit raised his brow. "Now, that *is* a story … Let's just say, there've been property disputes and it has changed hands. The Elliots couldn't keep up with the increasing expenses and Jackson Beauregard's company bought it. It's been sitting idle like that ever since."

"Why didn't he do anything with it?" I asked.

"Don't know. You'd have to ask him. I'm guessing he wanted to buy out the whole block for some future development but that never transpired."

As we chatted, the gala seemed to fade into the background. Our conversation flowed with ease and comfort. We stood shoulder to shoulder and people-watched. Whit slipped in nuggets about the guests.

I looked at the grandfather clock. "It's almost seven o'clock. They should be opening the parlor soon."

A sudden scream and commotion came from across the room.

"What was that?" Whit asked, looking toward where the scream came from.

The music stopped. Gasps and whispers rippled through the crowd. Amid guests shuffling about to either get closer or away from the parlor doors, Whit took my hand and pulled us toward the hubbub to investigate. I must admit, I was grateful he didn't leave me standing alone.

Whit tapped the shoulder of one of the men gathered around the entrance to the parlor. The very parlor where the Magnolia Rose necklace and other family heirlooms were on display. "What happened?"

"We have no idea. But it reeks of foul play." The man's hushed whisper sent a familiar chill up my spine.

Nellie Pritchett, the town clerk and official know-it-all, came bustling out of the parlor, frantically scanning the guests until her gaze landed on me.

"Oh, there you are! Excuse me, pardon me ..." She pushed through the crowd, patting her brow with a cloth napkin, and grabbed my arm. "Parker, you must come right away!"

I dug my heels and forced her to stop, which wasn't an

easy feat. "What exactly happened and why do you need me?"

"Oh, Parker. Tate Beauregard is dead. And the Magnolia Rose is gone!"

I wasn't sure if Nellie was more upset about the loss of life or the necklace.

Whit stepped into the conversation. "Why do you need Parker?"

Nellie snipped out a short breath. "She's a big-time crime podcaster!"

"Former," I corrected.

"We need your expert opinion. You know what to look for in a crime scene. We could use your help! This is similar to that one case ... 'The Heist from the Tropics: An Artifact Affair.'"

Clearly, Nellie had been busy listening to my podcast episodes.

Whit gave me an impressed nod. "Well, you better get in there and see what happened."

Before I could argue, Nellie nearly jerked my arm out of its socket as she yanked me away from the crowd.

When I stepped into the parlor, it was like entering a museum of antiquities. The scent of pine overwhelmed my overly sensitive nostrils. But there was an underlying aroma I couldn't quite place. It reminded me of marinara sauce or pizza, and it was the first time I had smelled it since I'd arrived. The large room was adorned with display showcases, fancy furnishings and exquisite tapestries. But the weight of tragedy hung in the air. My heart lurched as I took in the scene before me. A young man's body lay lifeless on the floor. No matter how many gruesome stories I'd dissected and parsed, I would never become desensitized to the shock of seeing an actual dead body. From my years of experience, I had no doubt that Tate Beauregard had been murdered and that the incident had taken place within the last five to ten minutes.

"What time is it?" I asked Nellie.

She looked at her watch. "Two minutes and thirty-two seconds before seven."

A few of the staff rushed about, their voices a jumble of fear and confusion, doing what they could to keep the guests from entering the parlor. A growing sense of unease rose in me as I scanned the room, looking for any evidence or clues left behind. I saw the broken glass case where the Magnolia Rose necklace had once been displayed, its absence obvious against the backdrop. It had been snatched away, and I assumed in the chaos of that crime, Tate Beauregard had ended up the victim of murder. A large bronze statue of what looked like a Roman gladiator lay toppled over next to the display case.

A part of me wanted to flee the room, leave behind the murder scene and refocus on the business of continuing my pleasant conversation with Whit Hawthorne, but the trajectory of the night had shifted. I had been drawn back into the world of crime. My instincts kicked into high gear. And though I had never worked a fresh murder scene on my own, I knew we needed to secure the room to preserve the integrity of the investigation.

"Get the staff out of here. And don't let anyone else enter this room. We need to prevent any further contamination of the scene. And someone should call the local authorities."

Nellie blurted out, "I already called. Sheriff Sinclair is on her way!"

I moved closer to the body to examine the scene. The woman of the house, Evelyn Beauregard, pushed her way toward me. Her sparkling gown now looked out of place against her grim but stoic despair.

"I'm Evelyn Beauregard. That's my youngest son dead on the floor. Who exactly are you?"

"I'm very sorry for your loss," I said.

"Thank you. But who are you?" The woman didn't bat an eye.

Nellie Pritchett butted in. "This is Parker Hayes from the podcast *Criminally Yours*. I thought she could help out until Amelia arrives. She could perhaps even assist with the investigation."

Evelyn Beauregard unblinkingly looked at me but spoke to Nellie. "If Sheriff Sinclair is on her way, we don't need additional help. Amelia's perfectly capable of handling this. We certainly don't need any ... *podcasters* meddling in our affairs."

Nellie brushed Evelyn's arm. "Oh, but Evelyn, surely Amelia will appreciate the assistance. It's not like this sort of thing happens in Magnolia Grove every day. Parker could offer valuable insight."

Evelyn Beauregard studied me up and down. She could cut through glaciers with those eyes. Again, she addressed Nellie. "We won't need any additional insights. I think it's pretty obvious what has happened here. My son died while trying to protect our Magnolia Rose."

"I didn't mean to intrude," I said. "I just wanted to make sure we preserved the scene, and any evidence."

The doors to the parlor shot open, and a frenzied young woman with a crown of blonde curls piled high rushed over to where we stood.

"What happened, Mother? What happened to Tate? Is he …"

"Yes, Annabelle. Our beloved Tate has departed." Evelyn kept her chin held high.

"Ohnoohnoohno!" Annabelle wailed as she knelt closer, mascara and tears streaking her pale cheeks.

"Get a hold of yourself, Annabelle," Evelyn said, her teeth clenched.

"But Mother …"

Annabelle lifted herself and leaned against her mother's firm frame.

Evelyn acknowledged me with a sharp nod. "You may excuse yourself, Miss Hayes."

Over the years, I'd seen and heard of various reactions to murders, some more reserved than others. Evelyn Beauregard was definitely on the reserved side. Honestly, after meeting her, I was relieved she didn't want my help. Getting embroiled in the affairs of the Beauregard family seemed like a whole heap of trouble. Good.

Nellie Pritchett shrugged and escorted me toward the exit. "I'm so sorry, Parker. I thought, well, I don't know… It's so tragic. The whole thing."

"Yes, it's horrible."

Just before we reached the doors, a towering broad-shouldered woman with a sheriff's windbreaker and badge marched in. Her hair was tied back so tight it looked painful. I assumed this was Sheriff Sinclair.

She scanned me up and down and directed her question to Nellie. "Who's this?"

"Parker Hayes. She's new in town." Nellie didn't mention anything about my "expert insights" or my podcast.

The sheriff raised her angular brows. "Well, both of you need to exit the room so I can secure the area."

Two more deputies trailed in, and Sheriff Sinclair began giving instructions. Though the no-nonsense sheriff displayed control and authority, I recognized the distress behind her eyes. Maybe from lack of experience or perhaps it was knowing that navigating the trail that lay ahead would be challenging. Probably both.

As I turned to leave what I was calling a murder scene, an uneasy feeling crept over me—the nagging suspicion that this wouldn't be my last involvement with the Tate Beauregard investigation.

CHAPTER 3

While the townspeople were busy gossiping on every street corner the days following the murder of Tate Beauregard, I spent the weekend knee-deep in dust, crumbling plaster and broken glass. Now it was the start of the week, and my building still needed a lot of work. The old drugstore had seen better days, and though Clyde, the teddy bear of a handyman, assured me it was all fixable, when he handed me the estimate, my heart clenched up. The costs were well over my already tight budget.

I gazed at the sheet of paper with multiple line items. "Well, this is unfortunate."

"She's gonna require some foundation work. That's where a chunk of the money will go."

I liked how Clyde referred to the building as a "she" and wondered if "she" would end up putting me in the poor house.

"That's not something we want to skimp on. And I say

that based on my experience watching home reno shows," I said.

"You're right on the button there, ma'am. Unless you want to risk the building crumbling in on itself."

"You mean more than it already is?"

I scanned the room, looking for a solution amidst the dust, debris and random junk strewn about. What a disaster I had not only stumbled into but paid for! I felt a rising anger toward the commercial real estate agent for selling me the bag of goods, but at the end of the day, I was the one who had signed the paperwork. In retrospect, doing everything online and rushing the process had been a mistake. I wasn't in the best frame of mind when I made my plans to leave the big city and relocate to Magnolia Grove. Desperate measures and all that ... All the non-stop traffic and pollution and crime and noise had finally pushed me over the edge. So, it was either a small town or a mental health facility. The pictures of available space in Magnolia Grove had more allure than the mental health facility, so I opted for that option. Then came the idea of opening my own cafe, and that vision seemed much more hopeful than studying, digesting, investigating and talking about yet another horrible crime. Perhaps I had stepped into a seemingly impossible situation, but I needed to trust it would work out.

I looked at Clyde. "Maybe I could help? At least with the demo and some of the smaller things that don't require a license or working knowledge of rebuilding foundational structures."

"Sure, you could roll up your sleeves and help here and there, but it ain't gonna make much of a dent in the costs."

I sighed, feeling the crumbling walls closing in on me.

"We could do it in phases. Start with the cafe, then do the upstairs apartment later."

"It's not ideal, but it sounds like my only option. I don't want to apply for a loan or borrow money from my parents."

"Understandable."

I stared at the estimate again. "I underestimated this venture. I guess living here during the reno is out of the question."

Clyde took off his ratty cap and rubbed his forehead. "Not while this bottom level is out of code. You could stay in my guest cottage free of charge. It's a bit small, but free is a lot cheaper than staying at the Garden Inn."

"Free sounds like music to my ears."

"Well, Parker, I'd say we've got our work cut out for us. Let's get going on cleaning out the old junk."

Not one to dawdle, I got right to it and began carrying what I could heave ho out to the dumpster Clyde had procured.

Ten trips to the dumpster later, and still knee-deep in rubble, Clyde and I took a short break to catch our breath. He handed me a bottle of water, and we sat on some overturned crates, surveying the mess.

Clyde took a sip of water. "Slowly but surely, we'll get there. I was thinkin', if you need any furniture or stuff for your place, you should visit Bennett's Antiques. It's just up Main, past Danny's Barbershop."

I raised a brow. "I think I've passed by it. Is that the cluttered place with all the old furniture and knick-knacks piled up?"

"That's the one," Clyde chuckled. "Lila and her brother Emmett run it. They're both a bit quirky, but they've got an eye for hidden gems."

"I could definitely use some unique stuff to give the cafe a bit of character. Maybe I'll stop by and see what they have."

"The Bennetts have been around forever. The family has been collecting from estate sales and auctions for well over a century. Lila's always got some interesting pieces in their shop. Just be careful not to get lost in there. The place is a maze of history."

I laughed. "I'll keep that in mind. Thanks for the tip."

We pulled ourselves up and resumed our work. Me lugging semi-heavy pieces of busted-up building and broken chairs, Clyde hammering into a plaster wall across the room.

Suddenly a crash of debris and rubble rattled the air. I turned quickly, my heart skipping a beat, and saw Clyde emerging from a cloud of dust, coughing and waving a hand in front of his face.

"Clyde! Are you okay?" I rushed over to him.

"Yeah, yeah, I'm fine." He brushed dust off his shoulders. "Just a minor mishap with some of the wall. It ain't no thing."

I let out a breath I didn't realize I was holding. "You scared me half to death."

Clyde's round face broke into a reassuring smile. "Sorry

about that. This old place is full of surprises." He handed me a dusty leather-bound book.

I flipped it open and admired the neat penmanship filling the yellowed pages. "Looks like someone's journal. Are you sure you're okay?"

"I'm fine. Bet you could find some good stories in those pages."

"I would imagine so. Wonder if the previous owner left it as an omen ... You know, like 'beware all who enter this building for it will crumble to the ground' or something like that." I snapped it shut.

Clyde rested his hand on my shoulder. "Don't be so glum, sweetheart. It's fixable."

"Ha! At a steep cost." I glanced around at the shambles that was supposed to be my cafe. "Seems like Catch You Latte is going to open a whole lot *latte* ..."

"Heh, the good news is, we can take down this hideous ceiling and keep the pipes exposed. It looks good up there. That'll cut costs."

I gazed up into the hole and had to agree with Clyde: the exposed pipes and rafters would give the cafe a bit of a rustic vibe.

Clyde pointed at the journal. "You know, I bet Whit Hawthorne would love to see that old thing."

I blew some more dust off the journal and opened the cover again. In marvelous penmanship, written on the inside was a name and date: *Penelope B. Elliot, 1923-24*. I tucked it away in my bag. Sure, I would bring it to Whit. It'd be a good excuse to see him again.

Clyde nudged me. "Why don't you grab that other

ladder and help me tear down these nasty old ceiling panels."

"You've got the right idea, Clyde. Doing some demo will be therapeutic."

"Why do you think I'm always so chipper?"

"Because there are lots of old buildings in town that need to be overhauled?"

"You'll be okay, Parker. Like I said, this is—"

"Fixable."

I put on a mask and grabbed a crowbar. I began ripping out the ceiling tiles and found the work cathartic. My anxiety lessened with each yank and tear down.

"Excuse me, are you Parker Hayes?" a man's voice called out from behind me.

I turned to find a well-dressed man with slick dark hair and a smirk that seemed to hide a multitude of secrets.

I lowered my mask. "I am."

His cologne of sandalwood and leather was so overwhelming, I could taste it. It was a scent that smelled of old money and power.

"Well, it's nice to meet you. I'm Jackson Beauregard." He held out his hand, and I removed my glove to give him a firm shake.

"Nice to meet you. I'm sorry about your brother."

"Yes, thank you for your condolences." Beauregard scanned the shop and changed the subject. "It appears as though you've got quite the endeavor with this renovation." His voice was low and serious.

"Yes. It would seem so. And what brings you here, Mr. Beauregard?"

He stepped closer, his gaze roaming over the mess. "Thought I'd come by to see your plans for the property. It was one of ours until your purchase. Honestly, I was shocked it sold."

I crossed my arms, trying to control my frustration. "You sold this place knowing its condition, Mr. Beauregard?"

"My company sold it."

"I suppose you don't mind that your company didn't disclose specific details like needing a new foundation."

"I don't manage those sorts of things."

"Hmmph."

In the back, Clyde let out a shout, and a loud tumbling crash followed.

"I'm okay!" He yelled from behind yet another cloud of dust.

"I better get back to work," I said.

Jackson's grin straightened out. "I came by because I'd like to make you an offer, Miss Hayes."

"You mean, you're willing to cancel the sale and refund my money?"

His laugh came off as calculating and conniving. "We both know that's not possible. But perhaps I can provide some financial means for your renovations."

"And what makes you think I need any means?"

"Let's be honest, you bit off more than you could chew."

Despite my reservations, my curiosity had gotten the better of me. "I guess it wouldn't hurt to hear your offer."

"I heard about your experience as a true-crime podcaster and spent the majority of the weekend listening to your show. You're not too bad. Then I did a background check on you and noticed you're a licensed private investigator. So, I'd like to hire you to help with the investigation of the murder of my brother, Tate."

That was an interesting twist. I wondered if he knew his mother, Evelyn, had dismissed my assistance the very night of the murder because she didn't want any help from me. Also, I wasn't exactly a "private investigator." I had gotten licensed so I could have easier access to information. That's one of the reasons my show was authentic.

I told Jackson, "My license is expired. And I'm a *former* true-crime podcaster. I'm done with all that."

"My instincts as a savvy businessman tell me that you have a keen mind when it comes to investigations and unraveling these sorts of matters. I'm not worried about licenses and such. Whatever information you need, I'll make sure you get it."

Wow. Jackson Beauregard seemed to have pull in this town.

"What about Sheriff Sinclair?" I asked.

"She's a barely elected greenhorn who's never been anywhere close to a murder investigation, except maybe in a book during her academy training. You have big-city experience with real detectives. I think we could benefit from an outsider's perspective. Look, Miss Hayes, I don't want this to drag on. My family wants closure."

"Speaking of your family. Um, your mother … She was pretty adamant about not wanting me involved."

"I'll handle her." He looked around the shop. "Of course, I'd compensate you handsomely for your services. And it looks like you're going to need it. I'm sure this is costing you a pretty penny."

"A lot of pretty pennies."

"Well, just think about it," Jackson said.

If I agreed to help with the investigation, I'd be reopening a door I'd already slammed shut and bolted. I was finished with murder and death. Coffee and sweet treats were to be my new passion. That was the main reason why I moved to this supposedly quiet town of Magnolia Grove. To start fresh and have a simple, stress-free life.

"I appreciate your offer, Mr. Beauregard, but it's going to be a hard pass for me."

Another loud boom followed by the sound of pipes clanking echoed through the shop.

Clyde emerged from the back, dripping wet. "Ahh, Parker, remember the quote I gave you earlier? We need to add plumbing to that list."

Jackson Beauregard patted my shoulder. "Here's my card if you change your mind." He turned to leave, then glanced back. "And Miss Hayes, I'd be careful with the second floor. It's a death trap."

CHAPTER 4

*L*ater that evening, after a long day of demo and the longest hot shower in the history of hot showers, I went down to the restaurant at the Garden Inn for dinner. The place reminded me of something out of a Hallmark movie with its cozy candlelit ambiance. The aroma of steak and fried foods filled the air. Centerpieces made of fresh flowers and flickering candles graced every table. Delicate music softly accompanied the bed of whispered conversations. I followed the hostess to a table, hoping the menu had my new favorite obsession—barbecued pulled pork.

"Miss Hayes," a familiar voice called out.

I turned to see Whit Hawthorne, the attractive and charming town historian. He sat at a table with a woman who appeared to be in her early forties. She had a slightly disheveled salt-and-pepper pixie cut framing her face, and she wore enormous black-framed glasses that magnified her eyes. Her kaftan showcased black and white geometric shapes, giving her a whimsical appearance.

Whit stood up, beaming handsomely. "Good evening, Parker."

"Hi, Whit. Good to see you again."

He gestured at the woman sitting at the table with him. "Parker Hayes, this is Lila Bennett. Owns Bennett's Antiques with her brother Emmett."

A tidal wave of rose-scented perfume washed over me as I held out my hand to greet Lila.

Lila shook her head. "Oh, sweetie, not to be rude, I really shouldn't shake your hand. I'm just recovering from a cold. You can never be too careful."

"Okay. Well, it's nice to meet you," I said, lowering my hand.

Lila continued blathering away. "I'm feeling much better. Thanks to my herbal home remedy. Listen here, next time you start to feel under the weather, you give me a holler, you hear? My remedy will get you right as rain in no time. It's been passed down for generations. Whit will vouch for me. Sick as a dog earlier this year. Fixed him right up. I'm babbling now, aren't I?"

"You're fine," I said. "And I appreciate your offer."

Whit gestured toward me. "Parker just moved here from the big city. She's going to turn Elliot's Drugs into a cafe. She'll be our local coffee connoisseur."

"Oh, that's great! We could use some good coffee around here. What do you think of Magnolia Grove so far?"

"It's nice. A bit more eventful than I was expecting."

Lila looked perplexed.

Whit chimed in. "She's probably referring to the murder of Tate."

"Goodness gracious. Yes, tragic. I hope it doesn't make you think poorly of our fine town." Lila looked down at her lap.

"I suspect this one was an anomaly for a place like this," I said. "But murders can and do happen anywhere."

Whit pulled out a chair and changed the subject. "Why don't you join us? Lila was telling me about some of the items she's going to sell at the next auction."

"I don't want to intrude," I said.

Lila moved her oversized bag from the table to make room for me. "Silly goose, you're not intruding at all! Please sit." She waved at the waiter. "Oh, waiter, another sweet tea for our guest. You do like sweet tea, don't you? Of course you do."

I looked at Whit again, and he gestured to the chair.

"Um. Sure." I sat down and turned to Lila. "So, Clyde Honeycutt told me about your antique shop, Lila. I'll have to stop by sometime."

"Yes, yes, please do come by the shop! You never know what you'll find, or what will find you." Lila's eyes twinkled.

She began rummaging through her oversized bag, muttering to herself and taking out random objects like a couple of eyeglass cases, a few tubes of lipstick and a book-sized lock-box. She returned everything to the bag.

"Everything okay?" Whit asked Lila.

"Actually, I just remembered I told Emmett I'd meet

him to discuss the auction items. And I need to give him a few things to take up to the cabin." She began rooting through her bag again. "Where are my keys … I can't find anything in this monstrosity. Good heavens."

She dug around in the bag some more. Whit and I exchanged glances and held back our amusement. Finally, she brandished an enormous set of keys that looked like they belonged to a custodian.

"Oh, here they are!" Lila stood up and draped her bag over her shoulder. "Well, Parker, it was a pleasure meeting you. Please come by the shop anytime! And Whit, I'll see you soon."

"Sounds good," Whit said.

"Nice meeting you." I waved.

"Have a lovely evening, the two of you." Lila gave me a knowing wink, then sashayed off, leaving a trail of rose-scented perfume in her wake as she exited the restaurant.

The scent of roses faded. I noticed a change in Whit's demeanor. His earlier charm seemed to have dimmed, replaced by a pensive look.

"She's a sweetheart. A bit flighty, but a dear." His stare was distant. "It might not have seemed it, but she's shaken up about what happened at the gala. We all are."

"I bet. Murder in a small town. Were they friends?"

Whit ran a hand through his thick hair. "They were on friendly terms. Which is saying a lot, given the long-running feud between the Bennetts and the Beauregards. Lila wanted no part of it though." He paused, his voice softening. "Tate and I … we were close once. Grew up together, actually. Drifted apart in recent years, but still ... it's hard to believe he's gone."

"I'm sorry, Whit. I can't imagine how difficult this must be for you."

"Stiff upper lip, as they say. Tate wouldn't want us moping around."

I gave him a moment before gently steering the conversation. "You mentioned a family feud with the Bennetts and Beauregards. Sounds intriguing. Like the Hatfields and McCoys?"

"I don't even know how and when it began, and I'm the town historian. I'm pretty convinced that they don't even know anymore. It had become a tradition. Lila and Emmett's parents were the last remaining vestiges of that nonsense."

"Wow. I guess when something goes that far back, it's hard to change. Speaking of town history stuff ... Clyde found an old journal from the 1920s hidden away behind a wall that caved in earlier today. He thought you, being the town historian, might be interested in seeing it."

Whit chuckled, then caught himself. "A wall caved in?"

"Yes, I'm pretty sure the whole place is going to cave in."

He tried not to laugh. "I'm sorry. That's not funny. I know the place isn't what you expected."

"I've passed the regret stage and now I'm in the acceptance phase. Maybe I'll have a T-shirt made: *I Bought This Ramshackle Building and All I Got Was This Old Journal.*"

"At least you've got a sense of humor about it."

"Many top psychiatrists say a good sense of humor is key."

"Doesn't hurt. Well, I'd love to see the journal. I can stop by, or you can bring it to my office."

"I'll swing by tomorrow between sledgehammering and bulldozing. I'd like to see where town historian Whit Hawthorne works. We better read the menu. The waiter keeps looking over here."

Whit handed me a menu with cursive handwriting and no prices. Always an indication that things would be expensive. Since money for extravagant dinners wasn't in my budget, I pinpointed what I thought would be the least expensive item.

The waiter, dressed in a white jacket and black tie, set a glass of sweet tea in front of me and then asked if we were ready to order.

"Yes, we are." Whit gestured toward me.

"I'll have the mixed green salad."

Whit shook his head. "No, no. You've been working hard. You need to eat. Bring her a steak." Whit looked at me. "You eat steak, don't you?"

I hoped the candlelight would mask my rosy cheeks. I usually wasn't so self-conscious in the company of men, but I was flustered around Whit.

"Actually … I'm currently having a love affair with North Carolina barbecued pulled pork."

Whit handed the menus to the waiter. "Very well. Two pulled pork platters with mashed potatoes collard greens and a side of warm biscuits. Sound good?"

I swallowed. "Perfect."

Whit took a sip of his sweet tea.

"So, Parker …"

I took a sip of my sweet tea, and wow, it was *really* sweet. "So, Whit…"

"Remind me, what brought you to Magnolia Grove of all places? We're just a speck of dust on a map. I'm not sure we're even on most maps."

"What brought me here? You mean besides escaping the noise, pollution, lack of parking, crowded places, prices and crime?"

"Yeah … besides all that. I suspect there is more to Parker Hayes than meets the eye."

I exhaled softly, debating whether or not to get into deeper reasons why I left the big city to start over in a small town. I was trying to let go of the past. But not one to keep secrets, I decided to give Whit a few breadcrumbs.

"Here's a more detailed tidbit. Let's just say one of my podcast listeners upgraded from fan to super stalker."

Whit's brows rose, and a genuine look of concern spread across his face. "Oh boy."

I stared at the flickering candle. "Yeah. It was creepy. But it's over and done with. Honestly, I've wanted a fresh start for years. The grind of investigating crimes and interviewing people for the podcast took a toll. My nerves were shot. But that's just part of it."

Whit sat quietly and listened. I was starting to appreciate that quality about him. He didn't feel the need to fill the silence with empty words, and the silence didn't feel uncomfortable. I liked Whit.

I continued. "The last time my parents visited me was about ten years ago. They got mugged, and after that, they were never going to return. And who could blame them? They are the sweetest people, and the thought of them getting robbed at gunpoint still haunts me. But it did jumpstart my career. However, the older I get, the more I long for a simple life. I love coffee and baking, and I'd like to have regular conversations that don't revolve around crime, podcast monetization, sponsors ... Most importantly, I wanted a place where my parents could visit without fearing for their lives. I would love to live in a place where my dad can crack his corny jokes without having to look over his shoulder, and Mom can go shopping without clutching her purse. Maybe a place safe enough for them to consider relocating to after they retire."

"You might want to hold off mentioning the Tate Beauregard murder..."

"Yeah. I'll keep that under wraps. Anyway, enough about me. What about you?"

Whit fiddled with his fork. "Oh no, I see an investigative glint in your eye. Are you about to go all podcast-host on me?"

I grinned. "I'm retired, remember?"

"Well, I refuse to answer your questions unless you do it."

I laughed. "Okay then, would you prefer I use my serious NPR voice or my peppy morning show tone?"

"Surprise me."

I cleared my throat dramatically. "Ladies and gentlemen, today on 'Parker's Hot Seat,' we have the elusive town historian, Whit Hawthorne. Whit, our listeners are dying to know: how does a dashing document-diver like yourself spend his days?"

Whit played along, adopting a mock-serious expression. "Well, Parker, it's a thrill-a-minute lifestyle. Picture this: I start my mornings wrestling with historical documents and dodging falling stacks of newspapers. By afternoon, I'm Indiana Jones-ing my way through dusty attics, searching for that one photograph that'll crack the case wide open."

"Fascinating!" I grinned slyly. "And your evenings?"

"Oh, that's when the real excitement begins," Whit said, leaning in. "I host underground timeline-building competitions. You haven't lived until you've seen two history buffs duke it out over the correct date of the town's first cow-tipping incident."

We both burst into laughter, drawing curious glances from nearby folks.

"Seriously though. It's a lot of research, community engagement, and yes, the occasional dusty attic adventure. But I love every minute of it."

"It sounds like you do," I said, my smile genuine. "Thanks for being such a good sport."

"Anytime." Whit raised his glass in a mock toast. "Just promise me I'll get a signed copy of the transcript."

"I'll email you." I eased back into my chair. "It sounds cool. Preserving history is important. You know what they say ... Those who can't remember the past— "

"Are condemned to repeat it."

"In a sense, our jobs are ... were ... similar," I said.

"That's true. Like an archeologist digging around in the details to sort out the real story."

"Although, I suspect I've dealt with the more gruesome aspects of humanity."

Whit took another sip of his sweet tea and grinned. "Oh, you'd be surprised at some of the stories I've heard. You wouldn't believe what people did with chamber pots back in the day."

The waiter approached our table and placed down our platters and a basket of warm biscuits. The pleasant scent of barbecue wafted between us. We dug in and savored each bite.

I took a biscuit, tore it in half and spread butter down the middle. It melted into the nooks and crannies. I took a bite and closed my eyes. "I could get used to this."

Whit set down his fork. "So, I'm curious. Do you have any thoughts on the Tate Beauregard case?"

"I hadn't given it much thought until today when Jackson Beauregard came by the building and offered to hire me to help with the investigation."

"Jackson wants to hire you? Really?"

"Apparently, he listened to my podcast and thinks I have a keen mind for solving crime. Which I do in theory, I guess."

Whit took a bite of his pulled pork and spent a moment deep in thought. "So, did you say yes?"

"No. Even though his payment would probably cover a bunch of my ever-growing renovation costs. I moved here for a new beginning. And honestly, I don't want to take his money for a job that belongs to the sheriff."

Whit grinned. "Understandable. I wouldn't want to get entangled in that mess either. Although, in my humble opinion, I'll bet you are a top-notch amateur sleuth."

"Thanks. Former top-notch amateur sleuth. Now amateur cafe owner."

"Soon to be top-notch."

AFTER DINNER, Whit and I took a stroll through the charming streets of Magnolia Grove. The moonlight cast a soft radiance on the cobblestone paths, and the breeze was refreshing.

As we walked, Whit's phone rang. He glanced at the screen, and his expression turned serious. "It's Sheriff Sinclair, excuse me." He held his phone to his ear. "Hello, Sheriff. What? Now? I suppose I could, I'm around the corner on a date … er … just had dinner at the Garden Inn …"

He hung up and turned to me, concern etched on his face. "Sinclair wants to see me at the station. She said it's urgent."

"Do you know why?"

"No idea. But I guess I'll find out soon enough. Well, Parker, it was a pleasure. You have a good night."

"I'm going with you," I said.

"I appreciate the gesture—"

I cut him off. "Gesture-shmesture. I'm going and that's final. Think of it as an adventure!"

Whit grinned despite the tension. "All right, if you insist."

We made our way to the one-story brick station a few blocks away.

When we arrived, Sheriff Amelia Sinclair stood waiting in the lobby, her composed facade giving nothing away. She noted my presence as a passing curiosity, like a moth that had fluttered in through the open door.

"Mr. Hawthorne, follow me," she pivoted on her heel.

Whit glanced back at me. "I'll be right back."

As they disappeared into her office, I stood alone in the lobby. I glanced around, taking in the stark, utilitarian decor of the station. It was as exciting as a bowl of plain oatmeal. The place was void of the hustle and bustle of every other police station I'd been in. My curiosity got the better of me, and I wandered over to the front desk, where a bored-looking older deputy sat reading a newspaper.

"Excuse me, do you have any idea why Sheriff Sinclair called Whit here?" I asked.

He shrugged. "Sorry, ma'am."

"Well, that's too bad …"

I paced around the lobby, wondering if the place was always so quiet, then concluded, yes, of course it was. The minutes dragged on, each one feeling like an hour. *What could be taking so long?*

After what felt like an eternity, Whit emerged from the sheriff's office, his face pale and stunned.

I walked over to him. "What happened?"

"I … I'm a suspect."

Shock punched my gut. "A suspect? In Tate Beauregard's murder?"

"Yes."

"Well, we know you couldn't possibly have killed him or stolen the necklace because you were with me."

"I told her that, but someone overheard Tate and me arguing before the gala."

"Arguing? About what?"

He stared off into the distance. "I'd rather not discuss the details ... But it was nothing. Like I said, Tate and I go way back. He was like a brother. At least he used to be before ... he changed."

I patted his arm. "I wouldn't worry about this, Whit. Sinclair probably thinks everyone is a suspect. That's the usual protocol. Cast a wide net."

"Yeah, I know, but I've never been a suspect in a murder."

Worry lined his face, and my heart went out to him. This wasn't the evening either of us had planned.

We left the station, and the streets no longer had that romantic allure. The streetlights now seemed harsh and the night air chilly. As we walked, I wanted to lighten the mood. "And the award for buzz-killer of the year goes to ... Sheriff Sinclair."

Whit let out a heavy breath. "Just another evening in Magnolia Grove, right?"

I linked my arm with his and bumped his hip. "For a small town, things are getting more and more interesting. Come on, let's get me back to the Inn. It'll be my last night before I move into Clyde's guesthouse."

"I hope you like dogs."

"Love dogs. As long as they don't bark incessantly."

We walked, and Whit's anxiety lingered around us like a dark cloud. I felt awful for him. I wanted to end our evening on a more positive note.

"You know, Whit, you don't have to worry. It'll work out. Besides, being a murder suspect gives you a certain ... mystique."

Whit managed a small smile. "Thanks, Parker. But I've never even been in trouble with the law before. This is all new to me."

"Well, reframe this now as a bona-fide mystery. Who knows? Maybe we'll uncover some other juicy secrets along the way. Like, who's been stealing all the garden gnomes in town."

Whit bumped my hip. "Thanks for making this situation ... better."

"That's my specialty. Well, sort of. Not really. Actually, my specialty is definitely not making situations better."

This got Whit smiling in the most adorable way. "I don't know how you do it, Parker. Turning everything into a pleasant bit of humor."

"It's either that or cry, and trust me, mascara streaks are not a good look on me."

We approached the Garden Inn, and I paused at the entrance, turning to Whit. Some butterflies fluttered in my chest, and I welcomed them. It felt good to feel something good. And exciting. I almost, but not completely, let myself swoon a little.

"Thanks for walking me back to the Inn. I'm going to

satisfy a bit of my curiosity tonight and flip through that old journal Clyde found. I'll stop by your office tomorrow to drop it off. Maybe that'll cheer you up. The journal. Not my visit."

Whit leaned down and brushed a soft kiss on my cheek. "Looking forward to it. The journal … and you. Parker, thanks for sticking by me."

I squeezed his arm. "Of course. Now go get some rest. This whole thing will blow over. You'll see."

I watched Whit disappear into the night, then headed into the Inn, my whole body buzzing with excitement. I hadn't received a kiss from anyone in a long time. Though it was just a simple peck on the cheek, I liked the idea of seeing Whit again.

I got to the room, changed into my pajamas and tucked myself into my comfy queen-sized bed. I grabbed Penelope's journal and nestled back against the pillows.

I opened the journal and skimmed through its pages of meticulous cursive handwriting. Its contents touched on a vast array of subjects that boggled my mind. Some entries contained shorthand notes about land transactions and properties, other entries looked like coordinates. Scattered throughout were snippets of codes and roughly drawn floor plans for the old drugstore along with some flowery poems thrown into the mix. My eyes grew heavy, and I started nodding off. Exhausted, I decided to leave the brunt of the decoding to Whit—after all, historians thrive on that kind of stuff.

CHAPTER 5

The next morning, I slipped into a pair of well-worn jeans, a comfortable t-shirt that had seen better days and my sneakers. I surveyed the three pieces of luggage that now contained my entire life, amazed at how easily everything I owned could be condensed into such a small space. Two bags held the mundane essentials of everyday life, but the third? That one contained the crown jewel of my possessions—a carefully curated collection of specialty coffees from around the world. I had a large enough stash to keep me supplied until I opened Catch You Latte and settled into my new life in Magnolia Grove. I had sold most of my other stuff before I left the big city. Even my podcasting equipment. I almost regretted that one, but I kept telling myself: *no, Parker, full commitment to your new life.* Eventually, I'd reacquire the basic necessities.

The kind people at the Garden Inn let me store my bags behind the reception desk, and I promised to pick them up later that day. They were sad to see me checking out so soon but understood my financial predicament. I couldn't justify staying there when Clyde had offered me a free place to stay during the renovations.

Before heading to the building to check in with Clyde, I decided to stop by Whit's office to drop off the old journal; perhaps diving into the pages of Penelope B. Elliot's riveting history would cheer him up, or at least distract him from the delightful experience of being on Sheriff Sinclair's suspect list.

I strolled across the town square, heading toward Whit's office in a restored bungalow he used as the historical society building, the bright morning sun warming my cheeks.

After a few short blocks, I stumbled upon the charming bungalow, which was nestled under the shade of a magnolia tree. I admired its picture-perfect postcard vibe. The front of the building along the porch had plaques commemorating various historical events. The rocking chairs added an inviting touch. However, as I stepped onto the porch, something felt a bit off. The front door was slightly ajar ... I pushed it open and stepped inside.

"Whit? You in here?" I called out, hoping to find him sitting at his desk with a cup of coffee and reading through old documents.

Instead, I was greeted by Sheriff Amelia Sinclair towering over the organized chaos on Whit's desk. She wore her hair in her trademark style, pulled back so tight it was giving her a face lift. Her badge was displayed on the front pocket of her beige uniform. The rubber gloves on her hands let me know that she meant business.

"Sheriff Sinclair? What are you doing here?" I tried to sound casual while my heart thumped.

Sinclair turned to face me, her expression as stern as ever. "Miss Hayes, correct?"

"Guilty as charged." I flashed a quick grin. "Where's Whit?"

"Mr. Hawthorne has been detained for further questioning."

"Detained?"

"Yes. Mr. Hawthorne is a person of interest in the ongoing investigation of Tate Beauregard's murder. As well as the missing Magnolia Rose."

"Look, Sheriff, I know he's on your list of suspects, but there is no way Whit should be a person of interest."

Sinclair's stern expression didn't waver. "Maybe for you he's not, but I have reason to believe he is."

I clenched my hands into fists to steady myself as the sheriff shuffled through some loose papers on Whit's messy desk and picked up a day calendar. She turned through a few of the pages, set it back down, then scribbled some notes onto her pad of paper.

"Is this about the argument someone overheard? That seriously can't be enough for you to detain him. Whit is an upstanding member of this community."

"Says the newcomer who has been here less than a week." Sinclair adjusted one of the rubber gloves on her hand.

I couldn't argue her newcomer point. Maybe I didn't have the full story on Whit, but I knew how to tell a good person from a murderer. Whit's behavior and demeanor had been calm and collected. I'd been around enough guilty parties to discern when someone was hiding something. I trusted my impeccable sixth-sense thingy, and not once had I felt uneasy around Whit. Not even when he got called in for questioning the previous night. Besides, he was with me at the time of the murder.

I glanced around, spotting papers and artifacts were scattered haphazardly. Drawers were open and books and trinkets were strewn about. Amelia Sinclair was making a mess of Whit's life. Literally and figuratively.

"Did you have to make it look like a hurricane passed through? Or is this just your signature style?" I asked.

"Look ... if you don't mind, I'm busy. You can be on your way now."

"Alright, Sheriff, I'll *be on my way*, but for the record—and you might want to add this to your notes—I was with Whit at the time of the murder."

She studied me with piqued interest. "Explain to me how you know the time of the murder."

"I've been around enough crime investigations to make a solid educated guess."

"Oh, that's right ... your little podcast hobby ..." Sinclair rolled her eyes and huffed.

"Little hobby? I do happen to have a PI license," I said. Which was true. But Sinclair didn't need to know it was expired.

"Look, I have some actual detective work to conduct, and your presence is not only contaminating the place, it's unwelcome. I don't need any outsiders playing detective and butting into my investigation."

Heat rose through me like I was catching on fire. "You know what I think?"

"What's that?" She folded her arms across her chest.

"That Jackson Beauregard might've been correct in his assumption."

"What assumption is that?"

"You are in over your head with this investigation!"

Sinclair's face flashed with irritation. "Be careful, Hayes. Your amateur sleuthing might get you into trouble you can't handle."

I was about to say something hokey like, "trouble is my middle name" but decided that might *really* set off the sheriff.

Instead, I turned on my heel and marched out, only half-regretting what I had said about Jackson insinuating Sinclair's incompetence. Hopefully, it wouldn't come back to bite me later. Knowing the likes of Sinclair and her uptight attitude, she'd hold it against me.

Whit detained? Ridiculous. Yeah, so he argued with Tate. That didn't mean he murdered the guy. And more importantly, *I was with Whit* when the crime occurred. Storming out of Whit's office, I made up my mind to take Jackson Beauregard up on his offer. I had my reasons: clearing Whit's name, proving Sinclair wrong (okay, that one was pure pride) and, I suppose, seeking justice for Tate Beauregard. The deck might've been stacked against me, but I had an ace up my sleeve that Sheriff Sinclair didn't—an outsider's perspective.

I ARRIVED at Jackson Beauregard's office, a little sweaty and a lot irritated from my charming encounter with the sheriff. Jackson's office was located in one of the town's more modern and polished buildings. The exterior, with its sleek lines and manicured landscaping, was void of any character. The place stood out like a cactus in a snowstorm compared to the historical charm of Magnolia Grove.

I took the elevator to the top floor—the third—where I found a receptionist who, after whispering on the phone with her boss, buzzed me into Jackson's office.

Jackson Beauregard sat behind his desk, looking smooth and groomed as ever in his tailored suit. He showed a playful smirk, but there was an edge to it, like he'd just won a bet. I felt a little underdressed in my jeans and t-shirt and my brown hair pulled back into a sloppy ponytail.

"Miss Hayes. I'm glad you decided to come." Jackson gestured to a chair in front of his desk. "Please, have a seat. I gather you've changed your mind about taking on the case. More busted pipes than expected?"

I sat down, crossing my legs. "Let's just say circumstances have changed. So, Mr. Beauregard, let's cut to the chase. You said you'd pay me to investigate your brother's murder. What's the catch?"

Jackson chuckled to himself. "No catch, Miss Hayes. Just a mutual interest in finding the truth. Sheriff Sinclair is out of her league. And that's exactly why I backed the incumbent Wade Tucker in the previous election. But I digress. I believe your unique perspective and skill set can uncover what Sheriff Sinclair cannot."

"Flattery will get you everywhere. But let's be clear—I'm not doing this because I'm broke and need to save my building from caving in. I'm doing this to help Whit Hawthorne, who is currently being detained for something I know he didn't do. I want to find the real killer."

"Understood." Jackson slid an envelope across the desk. "Consider this fifty percent of your retainer. The other half is to be presented when the murderer is caught and the Magnolia Rose recovered. I have no doubt you'll earn every penny."

I picked up the envelope and peered inside. There was a check with a considerable amount already made out to me. "I guess you're serious."

"One thing you'll learn about me, Miss Hayes: I'm always serious."

"I'm pretty serious too. For the most part. I mean, I'm not uptight or anything. Well, maybe sometimes. But I'm serious about my skill set, as you put it." I pressed my lips together to stop myself from rambling on.

"I know you are. That's why I reached out to you."

I squinted my eyes and studied him. "Admit it, you enjoyed my podcast."

Jackson began scrolling through his phone. "Like I said, it wasn't too bad."

"One thing you'll learn about me, Mr. Beauregard: I don't leave any stone unturned when I'm doing my research. Don't think for a second I'm going to let you off the hook if I find out you or anyone in your family is involved. Because in my experience with these sorts of cases, it usually hits close to home."

Jackson's stare didn't falter. "I would expect nothing less from you, Miss Hayes." He opened a folder and removed a piece of paper which he slid across his desk. A contract. I scanned it over carefully and took his pen to sign it, somehow wondering if I'd live to regret that decision. I slid back the signed contract and his pen.

"Excellent. Now, do you have any questions for me?"

"Yeah, I have some questions ... Where were you the night of the murder?"

He didn't flinch. "I was at the office. My receptionist can vouch for me. And so can the security cameras."

"Why weren't you at the gala? Seems like you'd want to be there since it was held at your family's estate."

I reached across his desk, grabbed the pen again and jotted down notes on the back of the envelope that contained my check. It was the only piece of paper I had on me at the moment.

"I wasn't there because I was vehemently opposed to having the event in the first place. But Mother insisted. She was dead-set on hosting a party and displaying that Godforsaken necklace," Jackson said with his aristocratic drawl. "Those events attract all sorts of unsavory characters, and frankly, I've had enough of playing host to society's backslappers. But when Evelyn Beauregard has a point to make, nobody better get in her way."

"What point did your mother want to make?"

Jackson leaned forward. "The same one she always wants to make ... that the Beauregards have been and always will be the most prominent family in Magnolia Grove."

I pondered his words for a moment. The quirks of the wealthy were often baffling and beyond my basic comprehension. But who was I to judge? I was now under the employment of one.

"What about Tate? Did any of those 'unsavory characters' maybe want him dead?"

Jackson turned around and stared out his floor-to-ceiling windows for a few quiet moments. "Tate had some hostile associates. He tended to owe money to lots of people."

"Why did one of the wealthiest people in town owe anyone money?"

"Let's just say my younger brother had a penchant for high-stakes gambling."

"I'll need names." I waved the pen in his direction.

"Well, you might as well look in the phone book of Magnolia Grove."

"That's helpful. Anything else you can think of that would actually be useful?"

Jackson turned around, his dark eyes narrowing. "I avoided the ins and outs of Tate's questionable choices. But I have complete confidence in your ability to find out what you need to solve this case."

"One more question."

"What's that, Parker?"

"What was he doing in the parlor before the doors were opened?"

"I don't know. I wasn't there."

"Do you have any ideas?"

"Maybe he was helping with last-minute preparations."

Jackson glanced at his office door, which I took as the end of our conversation.

I slipped the envelope into my bag and stood up to leave. "I'll keep you posted on my progress."

"I expect nothing less."

"I'll probably need to talk to your family, so you might want to give them a heads up. Especially your mother."

"Will do."

I left Jackson's office knowing two things. One, I'd have to stop by the Dollar Dash Discount to buy a notepad and pens. And two, I needed to stop by the station to review Sinclair's case notes. She might've been out of her league, but I had a hunch she was the type who took meticulous notes.

CHAPTER 6

After picking up a box of my favorite pens—black ink rollerball gel, of course—and a few pocket-sized notepads, I took the side streets to the station. I wanted to avoid the town square and the potential for small talk. I didn't want any distractions. Once I got on a case, I was like a dog with a bone. When I set my mind on something, all bets were off, which is probably why I spent nearly every waking hour on my podcast before I hung up my microphone.

I marched my way up to the station that housed Sheriff Sinclair's office, dripping sweat from the humidity. Stepping inside the refreshing air-conditioned lobby, once again I was struck by the stillness of the reception area. The only noise was the hum of the ventilation system. The bored-looking desk deputy from the previous night had been replaced with a young receptionist. She sat slouched behind the front desk, fiddling with her phone using her lightning-fast thumbs. Her name tag read: *Leigh Ann*

Fletcher. Her bleached hair was pulled up in a messy top-knot. Her mesmerized gaze remained on the phone screen until I strolled over to the front desk and cleared my throat.

She continued scrolling. "Yeah?"

"Is the sheriff back?"

"Not yet."

"In that case, I'd like to see Whit Hawthorne while I'm here."

I assumed Leigh Ann would give me something to sign, but she continued scrolling with one hand and pointed to the hallway with the other.

"Down the hall and to the left."

"I can just walk down there by myself?"

"Whatever. No one else is here."

This was definitely a small town. I shrugged and headed in the direction Leigh Ann pointed.

In an unprecedented first in my career, I came upon the small holding cell area unaccompanied. It held a couple of eight-by-ten cells furnished with a single cot. Whit was in the closest one, sitting on the edge of the razor-thin mattress and holding his head of dark, unruly curls in his hands.

"Whit Hawthorne. You have a visitor," I said in an authoritative tone.

Whit jumped up and came over, grabbing the bars like he wanted to pull them apart.

"Parker! Can you believe Sinclair locked me up? I thought you said not to worry. That everyone's a suspect."

"Clearly I underestimated Sheriff Sinclair's enthusiasm …"

He let out a sigh and cracked a grin.

"Everything's going to be okay, Whit. I just signed a contract with Jackson Beauregard, so I'm officially on the case. And I won't let it rest until we get you out of here and catch the real killer."

"I appreciate your help, Parker. And as soon as I get out from behind these ridiculous bars, I'll help you however I can."

"Two things you can do. One, try to remember if anyone else saw us talking together. Maybe someone took a photo of us. Any hard evidence that can prove you weren't in the parlor when Tate was murdered. Obviously, Sinclair isn't taking my word for it."

Whit ran his hands through his hair. He looked pretty good behind bars.

"While you're waiting, start thinking about motives for why someone would want the Magnolia Rose necklace. You know a lot of history about the people in town. Any insights could be helpful."

"The motive? Money."

"Of course … Not just the obvious ones. We're looking for underlying and sneakier ones."

"Like what?"

"Well, like my podcast episode 'The Monet Metamorphosis: When Art Theft Gets Weird.' Everyone thought it was a typical museum heist. Turned out the thief was an eccentric millionaire using famous paintings as wallpaper in his private bathroom. He called it 'living inside art.' Talk about a dual motive—greed and extremely questionable interior design choices."

"I really need to listen to your show."

"Former show. Anyway, while you're thinking on that, I'm going to hound Sinclair for her case notes and see what she has so far."

Leigh Ann's voice came from down the hall. "Sheriff's back."

"You good?" I asked Whit.

He shrugged and spread out his arms. "Living the dream."

BACK DOWN THE NARROW HALL, I made my way to the other end of the building, where I found the opaque glass door with a decal of a star and Sheriff Sinclair's name underneath. I knocked.

"Come in."

I entered her office. It was sparse and had moving boxes still unpacked.

She sat behind her wooden desk cluttered with files, a coffee mug and one of those hand-grip exercise thingies. On the wall behind her, the cork board had some mugshots pinned to it and a crayon drawing of a stick figure with yellow hair next to a house and a police car, signed in five-year-old penmanship, *Sawyer*.

"Parker." She stood up, all six feet of her, and gave me a frosty stare.

"I'm here on official business. First of all, Whit's innocent. You've got the wrong person."

Sinclair scoffed, crossing her arms over her chest. "Am I having déjà-vu?"

"As I've mentioned, I was with him when they found Tate."

"That doesn't mean he's not guilty. He could've murdered Tate and rejoined the party."

"He was with me for at least thirty minutes before they found the body, which was still warm when I entered the parlor. I believe the murder took place just before seven. If you could just confirm the time, I can find a handful of other guests who can corroborate we were together if you need more proof."

"That's privileged information."

"That's the thing. About twenty minutes ago, Jackson Beauregard hired me as a private consultant on the case."

"Private consultant, huh? Podcasting about crime is a different ballgame than investigating it."

"As I already mentioned, I do have a PI license."

"Yeah. Out of state and expired."

Ouch. Sinclair had been doing her background check on me.

"I'm in the process of getting all that updated," I said, bending the truth. "Look, I understand your frustration, but I wouldn't be here if I didn't know without a shadow of doubt that Whit Hawthorne is innocent. Don't you want to catch the real perpetrator?"

She sat back down and started shuffling through a folder. "You're wasting your time, and mine."

"I'm not sure Mr. Beauregard would agree."

Sinclair glared up at me for a painful moment, then

with much reluctance, handed me a folder with some loose papers. "I'll give you two minutes." She started the timer on her phone.

I reviewed the pages in double-time and scribbled down some notes of importance. Estimated time of death: just before seven o'clock. As I had presumed. Cause of death: blunt-force trauma to the head. Evidence of struggle. I paused and remembered the various statues in the parlor and the bronze statue toppled over. According to the notes, a loud crash around six fifty-five is what tipped off one of the staff to locate Evelyn Beauregard to unlock the parlor.

I looked up from the notes. "Do you think it could have been an accident? Like some sort of struggle where Tate was knocked down and hit his head?"

She pursed her lips. "At this point, I'm not sure."

"Do you have the murder weapon?"

"Nothing was found in the immediate vicinity."

"Do you know what it was?"

"We're awaiting forensics."

"Can you notify me when the report comes back?"

"If I remember."

It was clear I wasn't going to be deputized by Sheriff Amelia Sinclair anytime soon. I scanned the list of people she'd interviewed so far. All of whom were crossed off.

"You already questioned all the people on this list? And cleared them?"

"Mmm hmm."

"What about the staff?"

"As my notes clearly state, not even the staff had been

permitted into the parlor before the seven o'clock opening. Nobody had access to the room. Except for the family."

"And you questioned them?"

"That's what my notes state." She checked her phone.

"Does anyone know what Tate was doing in there?"

The sheriff shrugged. "Nobody noticed him go in. Nobody knows."

"Not even his mother?"

She shrugged.

I paged through the notes some more. "Ah-ha. The last few calls on his cell phone ... who are these people?"

Sinclair looked bored. "His bookie, a loan-shark and a pawn shop owner. All of them have airtight alibis."

I jotted all this down.

"Can you tell me who overheard Whit and Tate arguing?"

She inhaled slowly, then released her breath even slower. "Maggie Thomas."

"The owner of Boutique Chic?"

"Mm hmm. Your two minutes are up."

I sighed and handed the folder back to her. "Thank you for your ... help."

"Good luck, Miss Hayes. And a word to the wise: you'll want to tread lightly while you're digging up skeletons."

I gave her a half-grin, which was about as polite as I could manage, and left the office. After all the years of amateur sleuthing for my crime stories, I had never encountered such opposition from one of the supposed good guys.

NEXT STOP on my list was Maggie's shop. I entered the boutique to find the vivacious redhead whispering with a gentleman. Despite the summer temperature and humidity, he wore a three-piece suit. The gold band on his ring finger, the kind married men wore, caught my attention ... Maggie's eyes lifted when she saw me, and she quickly pulled away to come out from behind the counter. She plastered on a gleaming smile.

"Well, hello, Parker! What brings you to Boutique Chic this morning?"

I glanced at the man still leaning on the counter.

"Oh, this is Joe ... er ... Mayor Camden," Maggie blushed. "Mayor Camden, this is Parker Hayes. She's the one who purchased Elliot's Drugs to put up a much-needed neighborhood cafe."

I felt an odd churning in my gut as the mayor strode over to shake my hand. "Yes, I read the business plan. We're all looking forward to a decent cup of coffee in the coming months. Good to meet you, Parker Hayes. And welcome to Magnolia Grove. I'm sorry you arrived at such a ... dark moment."

"It's lovely here. Despite what happened at the gala."

Maggie and Mayor Camden gave somber nods.

"Just terrible." The mayor straightened his tie

"Just awful," Maggie added.

Camden glanced at his expensive watch. "I hope it doesn't stain your vision of our town. This sort of thing is highly irregular."

"It's practically unheard of!" Maggie said. "We hardly ever experience crime. Except for the occasional—"

The mayor interrupted Maggie mid-sentence. "Well, I better get going. Busy day at the office. Good to meet you, Parker. Stay out of trouble. And if you ever need anything, my office door is open for you. I am a genuine friend to our small business owners." He gave me a wink, which made my skin prickle.

"See you later, Joseph," Maggie said, waving him off.

He cleared his throat.

"I mean, Mayor Camden." Maggie blushed again.

After the door closed behind him, Maggie let out a sigh. "So, I'm dying to know … what do you think about Tate's murder? I'm sure you have some theories. Being a crime podcaster and all…"

I didn't have any theories at the moment, except that the town's sheriff didn't seem to have her own theories either. Aside from Whit being a person of interest.

"Funny you should ask, because Jackson Beauregard hired me to investigate."

"Well, I'll be darned!" Maggie absently shuffled through a rack of stylish summer dresses. "I guess he really doesn't have much confidence in Amelia. Can't say that I blame him."

"Why would you say that?"

Maggie strolled back to the counter and situated herself behind it. She loud-whispered, even though no one else was in the store. "Well, let's just say she's a newbie. She barely got voted in over the previous sheriff, Wade Tucker. Although it's probably best we got rid of him. That man was shadier than our oldest magnolia tree."

I took out my notepad.

"Wait, please don't write that down," Maggie said.

"I'm hoping maybe you could give some insight on what you think happened that night."

Maggie gasped. "Why do you think I would have any insights?"

Though her behavior hadn't crossed over into full-suspicious mode, I needed to take her off the defense, otherwise I wouldn't get any information out of her.

"Well, you were the one who reported overhearing Whit and Tate arguing before the gala."

Maggie seemed to ease back a bit and stared off for a few moments in deep thought. I remained calm as I waited for her to continue.

"It's true. I had to drop off something for Annabelle—that's Jackson and Tate's sister—before the guests arrived. When I was waiting in the foyer, I heard Whit yelling at Tate."

"Yelling? Whit doesn't strike me as the yelling type."

"Well, he wasn't exactly yelling, mind you, but talking rather heated."

"Did you happen to make out what they were saying?"

Maggie stared off again and played with her gold hoop earrings.

"It was something about money. And that Whit was very concerned about Tate."

"Concerned about what?"

"I guess Tate owed someone a lot of money and he

couldn't pay it off, and Whit was angry because he thought Tate might do something stupid. But that was all I heard, because Annabelle tapped my shoulder."

I scribbled a bunch of notes into my pad.

"Why were you meeting Annabelle early?"

"Like I said, I had to drop off something."

"What?"

"Her paycheck. She needed it that day."

"Paycheck? What paycheck?"

"Her paycheck! She works for me. Right here in my shop."

"Annabelle Beauregard works here?"

"For the last six months or so…"

"As I recall, it was you who told me the family is filthy rich. Is there any reason why Annabelle Beauregard needs to work here?"

Maggie began to fiddle with her necklace. "The family might be filthy rich, but not Annabelle."

"How so?"

"She's on a limited allowance. As a punishment of some sort."

"Very interesting."

Maggie applied some lip gloss. "She's great to work with. You know what her problem is though? She spends it as fast as she makes it. Maybe faster."

"Do you know why she was put on this limited allowance?"

Maggie shook her head in the most unconvincing manner. "Not really. But she came to work with me to make extra money. I must say, I was shocked when she showed up on Saturday morning the day after her brother was murdered. Poor thing. I begged her to go home."

"So, Annabelle came to work the day after Tate was murdered..."

"That's what I just said. I reckon she was still in shock. I'm sure of it. But she said she needed to get out of the house. Too many people and questions, and she just needed some space around the whole thing."

I wrote all this down, in shorthand, of course. It was clear I needed to talk to Annabelle Beauregard next. "Hmm. I think I'll go have a chat with Annabelle."

"Oh great! Would you mind taking her phone to her? She left it here."

"Certainly."

Maggie reached under the counter and retrieved Annabelle's phone. She handed it to me.

"Thanks for your time, Maggie."

"Sure. I hope you catch the killer!"

I exited the boutique, and right as I did, I heard the distinct "ping" of a message. It was Annabelle's phone. I instinctually looked at the screen and saw a message from Unknown. It read: *Piece is listed. Hope we fetch a good price ... See you at the cabin.*

I took a picture of the text with my cell phone.

CHAPTER 7

In the daylight, the Beauregard mansion was even more impressive, with its towering white columns, sprawling green lawns and the grandeur that shimmered under the golden sun. A silver Bentley was parked in the circular driveway, and behind it was a black sports car.

I walked up the front steps to the enormous double doors and rang the doorbell. It chimed like church bells and echoed over the solitude of the estate. I waited for quite a few moments before the front door finally opened and a lanky older gentleman, who I assumed was the butler, appeared.

"Hello, I'm Parker Hayes. I'm here to see Annabelle."

He stood off to the side, allowing for my entry into the grand foyer.

"This way."

I laughed lightly to myself, recalling the classic game of Clue: *the butler did it in the parlor with a candlestick.* In my experience, handling the heavy stuff with a touch of humor made it bearable. Otherwise, well, it would all be doom and gloom. Still, murder was no laughing matter. Since Sheriff Sinclair had already interviewed the butler the night of the murder, he was in the clear. He'd been busy assisting the guests as they arrived, and anyone could vouch for his alibi. Plus, he didn't seem capable of moving faster than a snail's pace, let alone murdering someone decades younger than him.

I followed the butler down the gleaming marble-floored halls and marveled again at the dazzling beauty of the Beauregard mansion. The decor was a seamless blend of antiquities and modern touches. It was just as stunning as it had been the night of the gala, but even more impressive without the guests.

We passed by the parlor, still cordoned off by yellow tape—a jarring sight in such an elegant setting. I made a mental note to visit the scene before leaving. Though days had passed since the incident, I hoped I could glean even the tiniest of clues. I'd seen cases solved with nothing more than a strand of hair or a button.

We stepped outside to a vast patio where a young woman with blonde curls and sunglasses reclined in a lounge chair under an umbrella.

The butler cleared his throat to announce, "Miss Annabelle. Parker Hayes is here to see you."

Annabelle popped upright and removed her sunglasses to get a better look at me. Her pale blue eyes were rimmed in red. She'd been crying. She extended her dainty hand. As I shook it in mine, I wondered whether such a small and delicate hand could be capable of murdering her brother.

"Pleased to meet you." Her voice was as soft and sweet as her appearance.

"Nice to meet you, although I'm sorry it's under these circumstances. My condolences to you and your family," I said.

"Thank you," Annabelle said, her voice tender. "I'm heartbroken inside, truly, I am. But have been taught to keep a stiff upper lip, no matter the storm. It's the Beauregard way." The last words came out of her mouth with a hint of sarcasm. She pointed me to a nearby lounge chair.

"Ring if you need me," the butler said, shuffling away.

I sat down and took out my notepad. "Thank you for agreeing to meet with me."

"Well, Jack didn't give me much say in the matter, so I guess I have to cooperate."

She rolled her eyes, reminding me more of a teenager than a woman in her late twenties. With the fairy-like vibe she was giving off, she seemed far too innocent to be capable of murder. But in my experience, even the most virtuous people can commit horrible acts, especially when driven by jealousy, revenge, fear or anger. In Annabelle's case, fear topped the list—the fear of not having enough money to sustain her extravagant lifestyle.

"Oh, by the way, you left this at work." I handed her the phone I'd been asked to return. I was glad my intuition told me to snap a photo of the suspicious text she received.

Annabelle took the phone, her eyes flickering with mild surprise before she quickly masked it. "Thank you."

"I just have a few things I want to go over with you."

"I wasn't even there the night of the gala," she blurted.

"Pardon me?"

"Well, I was there. But I wasn't there." She fell silent, as though this clarified everything.

"I'm not following."

She let out an exasperated sigh. "I was in the boathouse." She reached over for the pink lemonade sitting on the table next to her and took a sip.

I scribbled this down. "And why were you in the boathouse and not at the party?"

"I was planning to meet one of the guests to, um, show him, um, my boat."

Nothing about this sounded confident or true.

"Can you tell me who you were planning to meet?"

She shook her head, her curls bouncing. "Oh, no. I couldn't do that."

"And why?"

A rosy flush appeared on her cheeks.

I remained silent, waiting and watching for the dam to break and the truth to come rushing forth. Time ticked by. I was well-versed in sitting in uncomfortable silence, and I could see Annabelle starting to crack along the edges. I kept my gaze glued on her, exhaling slowly as if I didn't have a care in the world. Inside, I was tense with anticipation for what she needed to get out. Most people are terrible secret keepers.

She finished off the rest of her pink lemonade and slammed the glass down.

"Oh, fine! I was waiting for Emmett."

"Emmett?" I wrote the name in my notepad. "And is there a reason why you didn't want me to know this information?"

She sighed. "According to my brother, Jackson, the master of all things Beauregard, Emmett Bennett is on the list of men I'm not permitted to see. The Beauregards and the Bennetts are long-time rivals."

I remembered Whit telling me about the centuries-long family feud at dinner the previous evening.

"I see. Star-crossed lovers. Like the Montagues and Capulets…"

"The who?"

"Never mind. So, you were waiting for Emmett in the boathouse. Do you know what time this was?"

She closed her eyes for a moment. "It had to have been right around seven o'clock."

"How do you know it was around seven?"

"Because we planned to meet at the boathouse at precisely six forty-five. But I waited a little while, and when he still hadn't shown up, I ran back up to the house to see if he was there. Just as I entered the kitchen, Emmett grabbed my hand, and we snuck back outside. But we weren't in the boathouse long, because one of the staff called me back to the main house because … Tate was dead." She wiped her nose with her soggy napkin.

"Did Emmett say why he was late?"

"I didn't ask."

I jotted down some more notes and waited for the dots to connect in my head, then asked, "Did he seem like himself?"

"He seemed excited to see me."

"Did he appear distraught?"

Annabelle looked astonished. "You're not implying that Emmett Bennett had something to do with the death of my brother, are you?"

"I'm just asking questions."

"He would never, and I mean never, hurt anyone. He's the gentlest soul. He couldn't harm a fly. He's a vegan!"

I pretended to take down that information and instead wrote down that I would pay a visit to Emmett Bennett, the gentle vegan. "So, you still meet with Emmett even though your brother has forbidden you to do so."

"I can do whatever I want to do!"

"Is this why you've been put on a limited allowance?"

Annabelle gasped. "How do you know that?"

"Things are bound to come up during interviews."

"Well, since things are bound to come up, yes, it's part of the reason."

"What's the other part?"

"I guess I have a bit of a spending problem."

"I see. And what about your late brother, how was your relationship with him?"

Annabelle hesitated, her eyes flickering with emotion. "We had our ups and downs, like any siblings. I didn't even care when Mother promised him more inheritance than me last month. Deep down, we cared for each other. It's just … complicated. We both had roles to play in the family, and sometimes that created friction."

I decided on another line of questioning. "How are you

finding your job at the boutique? I imagine it's quite different from your usual social activities."

Annabelle sighed, her demeanor shifting slightly. "Oh, it's fine. I do enjoy helping people. It's quite … educational."

I raised an eyebrow. "Really? No frustration at having to work when you're used to a different lifestyle?"

She shrugged, appearing nonchalant. "It's a change, but I'm managing. It's not like I had much of a choice."

I made a few more notes. "One last thing, Annabelle. Is there anyone you know who might have had a reason to steal the necklace and harm your brother?"

Her expression darkened for a moment. "No one comes to mind. But then again, you never really know people, do you?"

I decided to bring up the text message and pulled up the photo on my phone. "You know, an interesting text dinged on your phone that I happened to see. My apologies for peeking, but I couldn't help it. It said, and I quote: *Piece is listed. Hope we fetch a good price … See you at the cabin.* Care to explain?"

Annabelle's face flushed again, but she quickly regained her composure and laughed. "Oh, that? It's just something between me and a friend."

"What friend?" I pressed.

"That's private," she said, her tone turning defensive. "Just a friend."

"Well, thank you for your time, Annabelle. If you think of anything else that might help, please let me know."

"Of course." She took another sip of lemonade.

"Oh, by the way, can you tell me the last time you saw Emmett?" I asked.

"The night of the gala."

"Not since then?"

"Well, he went out of town."

"Out of town?"

"Auction or something."

I found it extremely curious that Emmett happened to be out of town so soon after Tate's murder. And of all places to be, an auction. Perhaps trying to find a buyer for the Magnolia Rose necklace?

Annabelle picked up the little bell from the table and began ringing it.

I stood up. "Thank you for your time. I'll reach out if I have any other questions."

"Oh, one moment, Parker," Annabelle said. "You're not going to report this to Jackson, are you? The thing about meeting Emmett at the boathouse?"

"Like I said, these things have a way of getting out."

I left the patio and went back inside, waving to the butler as he shuffled by to tend to Annabelle.

BEFORE EXITING THE BEAUREGARDS' home, I made my pit stop at the parlor. Since Evelyn Beauregard kicked me out the night of the murder, I wanted to get a better assessment of the crime scene.

I ducked under the yellow tape and entered the spacious room. The art collection was a variety of historical artifacts, fine art prints, ceramics and statues, each piece different from the next. The crime scene had been somewhat cleaned up, aside from the broken display case that once housed the Magnolia Rose necklace. The glass box had been smashed. I deduced whoever took the necklace was either an amateur or in a rush, because smashing the glass wasn't exactly the stealthiest choice. A pro burglar would've been much more careful to avoid drawing attention.

I then examined the bronze statue, which was now standing back upright. The large Roman gladiator posed as though preparing for battle. Something about the statue looked off, but I couldn't put my finger on it. My cursory examination revealed no obvious signs of blood anywhere on the statue itself. But that didn't necessarily mean that the statue hadn't caused the blunt-force trauma. Obviously, there had been a struggle between Tate and the perpetrator since the statue had somehow toppled over that night. I searched the area for any looked-over evidence but found nothing of significance.

What I couldn't figure out was how the murderer entered and exited the parlor. The windows were too high up from the ground, and the only door into the parlor had been locked. When the staff person heard the crash, they needed Evelyn Beauregard to unlock the door to enter the parlor. So how did both Tate and his killer get in and out undetected?

"Ahem."

From behind me, someone cleared their throat. I turned to find the butler.

"The lady of the house has asked that you leave the premises immediately."

I assumed he was referring to Evelyn Beauregard.

"Does the lady of the house know that Jackson hired me as a consultant?"

"I can't presume to know what she knows or doesn't know, miss. What I do know is that she'd like you to leave now."

My visit to the Beauregard mansion was officially over. I shrugged and scribbled a few notes before exiting the parlor. As I left, I couldn't shake the feeling that Annabelle knew more than she was letting on. I also knew that my next stop would be Bennett's Antiques, where I would get the location of Emmett.

CHAPTER 8

⸎

Bennett's Antiques dominated the northwest corner of Main and Broad. The enormous building seemed to stretch endlessly. Large glass windows spanned the entire storefront so everyone passing by could catch a glimpse of the cluttered maze of antiques, knick-knacks and dusty relics inside.

I opened the door, and an inviting chime played a soft melody. Inside the shop, the overwhelming scent of apple-cinnamon potpourri attempting to cover up the underlying mustiness smacked me in the face. I didn't know which direction to go. There were three options. Straight and narrow, left and twisty, or right and tight. I chose the straight and narrow path and made my way down the aisle.

Teacups, possibly hundreds, lined the shelves. There didn't seem to be a system of organization to display the items. Everything was strewn about haphazardly. Undoubtedly there were treasures among the pieces, but it would take some serious sleuthing to sort through. We're talking more involved than the clearance section at a discount store.

I reached what I believed was the back of the shop and approached a long glass counter filled with more bits and bobs. A relatively modern cash register, plugged-in landline phone and a half-used receipt booklet suggested this was the check-out counter.

"Hello," I called out.

I stood there for a minute, then shouted a little louder, but nobody came to greet me. I wondered if the Bennetts had a security system because someone could've easily walked out of the shop with their arms full without paying.

I picked up a little bell from the counter and rang it.

A loud clang came from the back room, and a few moments later, Lila Bennett shuffled out carrying a large box of teacups.

"Oh, good morning, Parker! Or is it afternoon? What time is it? I've been in my own world sorting through a bunch of new merchandise …" She set the box down on the counter with a clatter.

"Hi, Miss Bennett, it's four o'clock."

"Please, dear, you can call me Lila." She wiped her brow with the sleeve of her bright yellow kaftan.

I gave her a warm expression, knowing I'd have to ease my way into this conversation. Judging from my read on Lila, she was a flighty and sensitive soul who could get easily flustered. I didn't want to put her on the defense right out of the gate.

"You'll have to excuse the mess." Lila gestured around

the store. "I've been trying to organize things, but we've just been so, so busy."

I looked around the cluttered shop, and something told me the place had been in disarray since before she was born. "How are you feeling?"

Lila straightened her oversized black-framed glasses. "I'm a hundred percent. My special cold remedy works miracles. You will let me know next time you're sick, right?"

"Uh, sure. I'll keep that in mind."

"So, are you looking for anything in particular? We have plenty to choose from! There's this charming set of mismatched chairs from the 1950s—they tell such a story! Oh, and the most darling art deco counter from an old soda fountain. Can't you just imagine the tales it could tell?"

Before I could respond, she was off again. "And the lamps! I have these delightful Tiffany-style lamps that would add such warmth to your space. Oh! And don't get me started on the vintage coffee grinders—they're not just decorative, you know. They're little pieces of history!"

I pointed to the box on the counter. "Well, I'll tell you this much, I'll be coming back for some cups."

Lila chuckled. "Yes, I have a wee bit of an obsession with teacups, as my brother Emmett likes to say. He says I'm a borderline hoarder. But sometimes I just can't help myself. I'm a collector of sorts."

I took that as my point of entry. "Is your brother here? I'd like to meet him."

Lila, in her quirky manner, swirled her hands around.

"Unfortunate timing, dear. Emmett is out of town at an auction. Unlike me, he loves to get rid of things. But he should be back in a couple days. The place is an hour's drive, but sometimes he likes to stay up there when he goes to the auction. We have a little cabin up there, though it's getting cluttered with more antiques. It's become more of a secondary storage than a place to stay. But I'm babbling now, aren't I?"

Lila looked curious when I removed my notepad and pen from my bag.

"Not at all. Where's the auction?" I asked.

Lila began taking teacups out of the box. "Oh, it's a little ways north of Magnolia Grove, right up Highway 39. Why …"

"Well, I was hoping to— "

"No, no, I'm not asking 'why.' *Why* is the name of the town."

"The town is called *Why*?"

"Yes, isn't that just the silliest thing ever?" Lila laughed.

"An hour's drive, you said?"

"Yes, a beautiful drive up through the foothills." She stopped sorting through the box and glanced over at me. "Are you planning to drive up there or something?"

"I'm thinking about it. I must speak with Emmett regarding the investigation."

"Investigation?"

"Well, yes. Jackson Beauregard hired me."

"Really? You're a private investigator?"

"Sort of. Let's just say I have a lot of experience in these sorts of matters."

"Oh, dear. Why do you need to talk to Emmett? You don't think he had anything to do with this whole … thing?"

"I'm talking to a lot of people. It's routine. Nothing to be worried about."

Lila's curiosity settled, and once again she went back to removing teacups from the box.

"That's a relief! Emmett is a tender soul. He wouldn't hurt a fly!"

"That's what I've heard."

She looked over at me, her eyes bugging out behind her oversized glasses. "Who else told you that?"

"Annabelle Beauregard."

"Hmmph! Don't believe a word that woman says. I've told Emmett to stay away from her. But he won't listen to me. Says he's in love. Madly and completely head over heels. He's just a passing phase for her, like a trendy hat, a pair of shoes or a purse. Bless her heart."

I continued with my subtle interrogation. "I understand there is some history between your two families. What's the deal with that?"

Lila picked up another teacup and began wiping it. "Oh, I don't let that nonsense affect me. But my mama, God rest her sweet soul, she loved to tell me those old stories. Like the time they tried to buy us out, offering us pennies on the dollar. And the rumors they spread, trying to discredit the Bennett name." Lila stopped herself and shook her head, her glasses slipping down her nose. "But that all happened before my time. It's ancient history, really. I'm sure my family played a part. It's not like us Bennetts had a squeaky-clean record either. We were rumrunners back in the day, you know? Bootleggers. Some of us moonshiners. For me, it's all water under the bridge, as they say. I just don't want to see Emmett get hurt, you see. Annabelle Beauregard can be very … finicky. I'm babbling again, aren't I?"

"Quick question. You didn't happen to see your brother after the gala, did you?"

"Oh, I was in bed asleep. That cold had me down for the count that day."

"I appreciate your time, Lila. I know you're busy, so I'll be on my way."

"Wait, before you leave. Here …" She reached into the box and took out a teacup with dainty pink flowers painted along the rim. "For inspiration. All of us in Magnolia Grove are very much looking forward to your grand opening."

I took the cup and slipped it into my bag. "Thanks. I appreciate the gesture. Right about now, I could use all the inspiration I can get."

I left Bennett's Antiques and headed down the street to my own mess of a building. I needed to check in with Clyde on the renovations and make plans for moving into his guesthouse. And I needed to find a way to get to Why.

∽

I ENTERED my shop to find Clyde talking to a couple of construction workers. He wore overalls and tall rubber boots. Large gaping holes in the old flooring exposed some of the underbelly of the building. My stomach tightened because I really loved those floors and was hoping we could salvage them somehow.

"Hello, Parker. I've had foundation crew here all afternoon," Clyde pointed to the workers.

"Whoa. You already got permits?"

"Nellie owed me a favor." He gave me a wink. "It's not as bad as I thought. We'll be installing some concrete piers under the foundation and supporting them with steel beams. Should be good to go in a few days. And don't worry about the floors. We'll patch them up like new."

Relief flooded through me and loosened up the knots in my stomach. Clyde was quickly becoming my hero.

"That's the best news I've heard in days. It sounds like you don't need me here at the moment, which is good because I'm going to be busy with some other stuff."

"So, you decided to work for Jackson."

"I did."

Clyde patted my shoulder. "I know it was a tough decision, Parker, but just think, you won't be in the red when this is all said and done."

He dug into the front pocket of his overalls and pulled out an envelope. My second envelope of the day.

"Here's the address and key to my guesthouse. My place is walking distance from town. You'll be greeted by Major. He's a feisty little mutt, but you give him a belly rub and some dog treats, he'll be your best friend. I left some in the guesthouse."

"Belly rubs and treats. Noted."

"Okay then. I put some food in the fridge for you and

left out a pecan pie on the counter. I like to bake in the evenings. Also, I have an old station wagon you can borrow anytime. Her name is Bertha. I left the keys under the sun visor." He winked.

"Are you the most wonderful human ever? This is incredibly generous of you. I'll find a way to pay you back. Free coffee and cinnamon rolls for life!"

"I'm more of a muffin man."

"Fine. Blueberry muffins for life."

We laughed, and for a moment, things were starting to feel hopeful.

"Seriously, though, Clyde. Thank you."

I detected a hint of a blush as he rubbed his white beard. "It's nothing. Just a few things to tide you over until you get settled."

"I won't be getting settled any time soon. Whit's been detained, and I need to get him out of jail. That's the real reason I took the case."

"Jail?"

"Sheriff Sinclair … It's a whole thing. Either way, he was with me at the time of the murder, but apparently my word isn't good enough. You saw me with him, right?"

"I sure did. In fact …" Clyde dug into another pocket, pulled out his phone and started scrolling through his photos. "Where is that … No, not that one … Oh, here it is. Look." Clyde handed me his phone.

I looked at the picture of Clyde at the gala decked out in his seersucker suit standing next to his friend Trent Ashworth.

"A picture of you and your buddy Trent at the gala?"

"Zoom in and look behind us."

I zoomed in and searched the background.

Bingo!

Whit and I engaged in a conversation, my head tilted back laughing and Whit grinning, as handsome as ever. I clicked on the photo and noted the time stamp.

"Well, thanks to you, I have irrefutable evidence proving Whit's whereabouts when the murder took place. Can you text me that?"

Clyde took back his phone and texted me the photo. My phone dinged. I snatched it out of my bag and clicked on his message. I saved the picture to my photo gallery.

"Thanks. I'm heading down to the station right now. After that, I need to get my bags from the Inn and head to the guesthouse. It's been a long day."

"I'll pick up your bags when we're finished here. Wouldn't want you dragging luggage through town."

"Clyde, seriously, you're an angel straight from heaven."

On my way out, I noticed a hole in the wall leading to a room I didn't remember seeing.

"Hey, Clyde. What's that all about?"

He walked over and gave me a big smile. "That, my dear, is a secret hideaway. It's where the Elliots hid booze during the days of prohibition. Rumor has it that's also where they stashed valuables."

"Were they bootleggers?"

"Among many things..."

"Interesting. Okay, well, let's just use it for the pantry or something. I don't see bootlegging or hiding valuables in my future. But at the rate things are going, you never know."

Clyde gave me a pat on the shoulder and went back to dealing with the foundation.

I exited my building and headed down to the station again. My home away from home, so it seemed. It was time to get Whit released.

∼

Inside the station, Leigh Ann Fletcher sat in the same slouched position behind the front desk. Her gaze remained trained on her phone, as though the fate of the world depended on the next text.

I approached and rapped on the desk. "I hate to interrupt you, Leigh Ann, but is Sheriff Sinclair available?"

Leigh Ann's eyes flickered up for a nanosecond before returning to her phone. "No."

Of course she wasn't.

"Is she here?"

"No."

"Do you know when she'll be back?"

"No."

I inhaled and released my breath. Patience, I told myself. "In that case, I'd like to see Whit Hawthorne."

She looked up from her phone. "Afraid that's not possible."

"Why?"

"Sheriff's orders. No visitors."

Maybe it was hunger or exhaustion or just straight-up

paranoia, but I was starting to think Sinclair was stonewalling me. *Maybe* it had something to do with my comment about her being in over her head with this investigation...

"Can you tell her to call me when she's back?"

Leigh Ann shrugged. "Okay."

"Thanks for your help, Leigh Ann. Your dedication to public service is truly inspiring."

"You're welcome." She went back to doing her phone stuff.

I departed the station and headed to Clyde's guesthouse. What I needed was some food, a shower and some rest. Then I'd be ready to take another swing at this piñata of a case, hoping that some more viable clues would spill out.

∼

CLYDE'S HOUSE was a modest craftsman style nestled in one of Magnolia Grove's oldest neighborhoods, just a ten-minute walk from downtown.

When I opened the back gate and entered the backyard, a furry bullet shot out from around a hydrangea bush. Major, the little black-and-white dog, came bounding up to me, barking and wagging his tail.

"Well, you must be Major!"

He stood on his hind legs and pawed at my thighs, saying hi to me.

"Nice to meet you, too."

I picked him up and carried him with me into the

guesthouse, which was a garage that had been converted into a spacious studio. The place had new pine floors, fresh paint, a kitchenette and a full bath. Clyde had even furnished the space with the essentials: a full-size bed, a small dining table, two chairs and a cozy reading chair. The kitchen nook included the basics like a mini-fridge, sink, toaster oven and a hotplate. It was the perfect setup while the renovations for my shop were being completed. And the best part... it was free.

I set Major down and gave him a belly rub, then a treat. I cut myself a heaping slice of pecan pie and sat at the table to review my notes from the day of interviews and plan out my next steps...

CHAPTER 9

The next morning, I woke up to sunlight pouring in through the window and Major licking my cheek. Not a bad way to start the day.

"Good morning, Major!"

I rolled out of bed and got my bearings. Sure enough, my luggage was sitting next to the front door. Clyde had made good on his promise.

Major hopped down from the bed and ran in quick circles around me, then stopped and looked up.

"I suppose you want a treat?"

He stared at me with very serious round eyes, his tail wagging back and forth. I tossed him a treat, then turned my attention to the most crucial part of my morning routine. I went to the luggage that contained my specialty coffees and grabbed a bag at random. Ah, Machu Picchu Morning, a single-origin Peruvian blend from a small, high-altitude farm in the Andes.

While the coffee steeped, the scent of citrus and toasted

almonds danced around the studio. I got a clean pair of jeans and a blouse from my luggage. I needed to look a bit more like a professional consultant and less like a t-shirt-wearing slacker.

I poured a cup, and the first sip was a revelation—bright, full-bodied, with a subtle sweetness that lingered on the palate.

Energized and ready to face a new day, I left the guesthouse and strolled down the pathway with Major shadowing me.

"Sorry, buddy. Can't bring you. I've got business to attend to."

Major stared at me for a moment, then turned around and trotted back down the path and found a sunny spot on Clyde's patio.

It wasn't difficult to locate Clyde's station wagon. Bertha, as he called her, was parked on the side of his cute craftsman home. The car was a 90s Buick Roadmaster with faded brown panels that had seen better days. I slid into the passenger seat. The interior smelled like leather and motor oil. True to Clyde's word, the keys were in the sun visor. When I fired it up, she growled, rumbled, then purred like a kitten. I shifted it into drive and headed to the station.

～

When I entered the station, Sinclair stood in the lobby talking to a deputy. I waited in the reception area until she decided to acknowledge me. She shooed the deputy away and turned to me. "Parker."

"Good morning, Sheriff. Another beautiful day in Magnolia Grove."

"I suppose you're here to strong-arm me into releasing Whit."

"First, let me extend an apology. I was out of line yesterday. I know you are fully capable of managing this case. I just can't help myself, I guess."

Sinclair eyed me suspiciously. I figured you could never go wrong with an apology.

"Anyway, I'm here to give you proof that Whit was with me during the timeframe that the murder occurred."

I held out my phone and showed her the photo. She snatched it and pressed on the photo to examine the date and time stamp.

She handed the phone back. "This could easily have been adjusted."

"It could have, but it wasn't. And if you zoom in and scroll over to the right, you'll see the grandfather clock."

I held out the phone and showed her the clock. Of course, I had scrutinized every pixel of the photo before bed. Now there was no denying Whit's release.

"Fine, Parker. I'll get started on the paperwork. Not bad, for an amateur."

I shrugged. "The clues are always out there just waiting to be picked up."

The sheriff smirked. "How's the rest of your investigation going?"

I thought long and hard about how to answer that question because I wasn't sure I trusted Amelia Sinclair. Not only because she presumed Whit was a person of interest. It wasn't even her coldness toward me. There was something about Sinclair I couldn't peg, and the fact that I couldn't bothered me. I rarely met a person I couldn't get some kind of read on.

After what seemed to be forever, Whit came walking out into the lobby with two-day scruff and wrinkled clothes but a broad grin.

"You did it, Parker. Thank you!"

He hugged me. It was amazing that after a night in the slammer, Whit still smelled like vanilla with just a hint of lemon.

I showed him the picture. "The truth is often difficult to refute."

"That's not a bad pic. Send it to me."

"You got it. Come on, let's get out of here. I've had enough of this place." I tugged his arm.

"Tell me about it. I need to get home and shower," Whit said.

"Do you think that could wait?"

"Sure, but why?"

"Come on, I'll tell you on the way …"

Outside, I pointed to Bertha and tossed him the keys.

"I think it's better if you drive since you know the area."

"Clyde still has this thing?" Whit laughed.

"Yep. And she runs smoothly, for the most part. Hopefully, she'll get us to Why."

"Why? Uh, okay …"

We got into the car, and Whit started driving us out of

town. I immediately took out my notes and began reviewing them again.

"So, are you going to tell me why we're going to Why?" Whit asked.

"An auction."

"Any particular reason we're going to an auction?"

"I'd like to find Emmett Bennett."

"I'm assuming this is about Tate's murder?"

"Mm hmm …"

"Hellooo … earth to Parker …"

"Sorry, I get a little obsessive when I'm organizing details of a case. But it always pays off."

"Okay, well, we've got about an hour's drive, so lay it on me. You know, tell me what you're thinking so far."

"Emmett Bennett killed Tate the night of the gala."

"Whoa. That's a pretty definitive accusation."

"There have been some developments while you were locked up. One, I found out Annabelle Beauregard has been put on a limited allowance and works at Maggie's shop. I can't imagine Jackson's 'allowance' and her hourly wage are enough to cover her lavish lifestyle."

Whit glanced over. "Everyone in town knows about that."

"Does everyone in town know that Annabelle and Emmett are secretly dating? And that Emmett is madly in love with Annabelle? In my experience, people madly in love can end up doing questionable and sometimes dangerous things for the other person."

I paused and scribbled down one more thought.

"Keep going." Whit turned up the AC.

"So, my theory is that Annabelle Beauregard persuaded Emmett Bennett to steal the Magnolia Rose necklace. Tate caught Emmett during the robbery. There was a scuffle that got heated, and well, in desperation, Emmett either bashed Tate over the head with something or shoved him into the bronze statue—or both—then took off with the necklace."

We were quiet for a few moments as Whit digested what I considered a pretty solid theory. I resumed. "Two things have led me to believe this. One, Annabelle received a text that, *Piece is listed. Hope we fetch a good price ... See you at the cabin.* Long story why I had her phone, just track with me ... The second thing is, Emmett left town immediately after the gala ... And he's at an auction. What happens at auctions? People sell things. Tell me that's not suspicious! And Lila mentioned he was at the family cabin, which is also mentioned in the text to Annabelle. Also, when I asked Annabelle about the text, she said, and I quote, 'It's just something between me and a friend.' When I asked who this friend was, she refused to tell me. My conclusion: robbery gone wrong."

"That is fascinating." Whit put his hand in front of the vent to see if the AC was working.

I closed my notebook and gazed at the dense forest of oak and pine trees that hugged the two-lane road. Their canopies created a tunnel of sunlight ... It was a beautiful landscape. "The only thing I can't figure out is how Emmett got in and out of the parlor. It was locked the whole time. I guess he could've had a ladder under the window, but the timing doesn't make sense, because he met with Annabelle. Unless …"

I flashed back to my building and walking by the hole in the wall the Elliots used as a secret room for their bootlegging operation and hiding away their valuables.

Whit and I both shouted, "A secret passage!"

Whit started banging the steering wheel in excitement. "Parker, you just opened up a blast-from-the-past memory! Tate and I used to play around in his mansion, and they had these little passages here and there. Guess where one of them went?"

"The parlor."

"The parlor! Wow … that was so long ago …" Whit suddenly got quiet. "He's gone … I haven't gone about processing that part yet."

I looked out the window as the forest of trees zipped by, not sure what to say.

Whit broke the silence. "Parker, what about you? Your childhood and all that?"

"You know. Typical. Grew up just outside the 'big city.' Precocious. Loved reading. Solving puzzles. Only child. Was always my dream to move to the big city, and when I graduated, I did. Made a popular podcast then packed up and moved here."

"Great bullet points. Now I really feel like I know Parker Hayes on a deeper level!" He chuckled.

"I know, I guess I don't like talking about myself. I think I'm pretty boring with a boring past. That's why I like asking the questions."

"If there is one thing Parker Hayes is not, it's boring."

"I'm pretty boring."

"Let's make a bet. If I can prove you are not boring, you owe me coffee for life."

"Coffee for you, coffee and muffins for Clyde. I'm going to be giving away all my goods! What do I get *when* I prove that I'm boring?"

"You won't win, because I am going to prove you wrong right now."

"Oh yeah? How's that?"

"Okay. So, you never told me much about why you left the city. Aside from the whole 'fresh start/fan-turned-stalker' thing, which, by the way, already disqualifies you from the 'boring' category."

"You mean everyone doesn't have their own stalker?"

"What happened? Some guy just started stalking you?"

"Well, there's a bit more to the story."

"We got time. Let's hear it."

"There was this one case, a high-profile one. A tech company head involved in some shady dealings. I dug up things that got him arrested. A listener, who had gotten fired from that company years before because he wouldn't do shady stuff, became my number one fan."

"Oh boy," Whit said. "I can see where this is headed."

"Yeah. At first, he just did fan-like stuff. Started a fan site, would promote the show everywhere and anywhere he could. He engaged a lot in the comments section on the show's site and defended my honor against any trolls and naysayers. Then he started sending me emails asking if we could do lunch. Then came the texts and voicemails. Finally, notes at my doorstep."

Whit grimaced. "Creepy. Did you ever find out who it was?"

"Eventually, yes. A techy guy who worked in IT. Used his skills to hack into my life. Knew my routines, favorite places, even what I was working on before I streamed it. The cops caught him trying to break into my apartment with micro-cameras. He claimed he just wanted to make a documentary about me. Well, that was it. My life had become an episode of *Criminally Yours*. So, I hung it up. And here I am."

"That's terrifying, Parker. You think he'll come looking for you?"

"Who knows? Maybe the few years in prison will change him. Maybe not. I'm not going to worry about it, though. Luckily, Magnolia Grove is far away from all that."

"Well, like I said, not boring ... I look forward to free coffee for the rest of my days!"

"Okay, I'll give you that. But after we prove Emmett Bennett murdered Tate Beauregard, I'm going to become boring Parker Hayes who sells coffees, teas and desserts to the locals in town. Count on it, Whit Hawthorne."

Whit was quiet for a moment before he glanced over at me. "I'm having a problem wrapping my head around Emmett Bennett as the killer. I grew up sort of knowing him, and—"

"Yeah, I know, he wouldn't harm a fly."

"It's not even that he wouldn't harm a fly, it's that if he saw a fly injured, he'd try to help it. He's on that kind of level."

"Well, one thing I've learned: people can be full of surprises."

CHAPTER 10

Bertha the station wagon lumbered into Why. The town unfolded like a miniature Swiss village transplanted into the Appalachian foothills, complete with gingerbread-trimmed chalets and flower boxes bursting with colorful blooms. At the edge of town, a massive red barn stood nestled against the mountains. Painted on one side of the barn was a mural that read "Why Not Auction House."

Whit turned into the gravel lot and parked. We got out and crunched our way over the small rocks toward the red barn. People were coming and going.

Inside the cavernous space of the auction house, the atmosphere hummed with anticipation, a mix of perfumes, old wood and excitement. Eager bidders from all walks of life filled the rows of folding chairs—local farmers in overalls rubbed elbows with antique dealers from the city, while tourists and seasoned collectors eyed the diverse array of items on display.

Whit grabbed an auction catalog. "So, what's the plan?"

"I think the best approach is casual and calm. Since Emmett doesn't know me, it makes sense if you introduce me to him. So, when you find him, we can just nonchalantly meander over to him and act like we're here for something else."

"Like what?"

"I don't know ... Make up something. You're here to bid on ... that giant blue-and-white vase I saw coming in."

"But that's a lie."

I elbowed him. "Well, consider it a tactic. It's only a white lie. Are you nervous?"

"I've never been part of a sting before."

"Oh, my goodness. You're hilarious. Look, all we're doing is asking him questions. It's not like we have the authority to arrest him. We'll take our findings to Sinclair, and hopefully she won't dismiss me this time. You ready?"

"Ready as I'll ever be."

We circled the perimeter and headed toward the location where the auction was in progress. The auctioneer, an older gentleman in a pinstriped suit, stood on a raised stage next to an oil painting and rambled into a microphone with a fast-paced and articulate cadence. He surveyed the crowd of bidders and pointed at those raising their paddles. Clerks stood around the edges of the area to record bidding information.

"Going once, going twice, sold!" The auctioneer's gavel hit the podium with a thud. "For twenty-five hundred dollars, the William T. Lansing equestrian oil painting goes to bidder 115."

I nudged Whit's arm. "Twenty-five hundred for that ugly painting?"

"That's nothing. Stick around. Some of these lots can fetch unbelievable numbers. And you wouldn't know why." Whit turned his attention back to the stage.

The auctioneer continued, "Next is lot 73, a beautiful late 19th-century antique decorative sword with bronze hilt and intricate floral motifs, recently restored, provenance unknown, anonymous seller."

I punched a mesmerized Whit on the shoulder. "Come on, Whit. This isn't history buff time."

"Sorry. That's a stunning piece. It looks familiar."

"I'm sure you've seen it in one of your books or something. You can study up on it later. We have a murder investigation to conduct."

We inched along the perimeter.

"Do you see Emmett anywhere?" I surveyed the crowd.

Whit studied each row, squinting as he searched.

He stopped and pointed. "I see him!"

I lowered his hand. "Nonchalant, remember…"

"He's over on that side, back corner."

I looked across the room beyond the audience until I spotted a slender man with a mop of salt-and-pepper curls inspecting an old-looking chair. "Let's go."

Whit took my hand, and we walked across the room. I thought his taking my hand was a nice gesture. We slowed as we approached Emmett.

Whit took the lead. "Emmett? Is that you?"

Emmett Bennett turned around. Like his sister Lila, he had large, inquisitive eyes and a whimsical appearance. He wore a yellow seersucker blazer lined with pastel plaid which matched his pastel plaid pants. Thin as a reed, he swam in the suit. I assumed it was the vegan diet.

"Hey Whit. What are you doing here?"

"Just, um, I heard about this event from, uh, a friend."

Originally, I planned to stand back and observe, but Whit's undercover act was evaporating by the second.

I held out my hand. "Hi, I'm Parker Hayes. I just moved to Magnolia Grove to open a cafe. I asked Whit to bring me by the auction to maybe purchase some items for my place."

Whit gazed at me with an impressed smile.

Emmett shook my hand. "Hey, yeah. I heard about the plans for the old drugstore. Looking forward to a decent cup of coffee. Didn't think anyone would ever buy the place. It's been abandoned for decades. Used to belong to my family back in the day."

That was shocking information. "I thought it belonged to the Beauregards."

"Well, yeah, one of my great-great aunts on the Bennett side married an Elliot. And then, well, the Beauregards got it from the Elliots. Anyway, it's a great location. I look forward to seeing the building restored to her former beauty."

Whit joined the conversation. "So, are you up here buying or selling?"

Emmett looked at his phone, then slipped it back into his pocket. "My sister wanted me to auction off a few items. I thought maybe the end of the world had come because if you know Lila, she's not one to get rid of anything. Ha ha."

I thought back to the state of the cluttered shop and her mentioning how Emmett called her a borderline hoarder. He had to have been lying. She didn't seem capable of letting anything go.

"What pieces?" I asked.

Emmett opened up the auction catalog and pointed to a listing with a photograph. "Right there, ain't she a beauty? That there is an 1875 Victorian pocket watch. It fetched twelve hundred dollars! I was only expecting six hundred, so this was a nice little windfall. I've got some other lots listed, but not nearly as exciting. Just some old military pieces."

"May I see that?" I asked.

Emmett handed me the catalog, and I flipped through the pages, glancing at the photos for his lots. I didn't think Emmett was foolish enough to list the Magnolia Rose in the catalog, but you never knew. You'd be amazed how often criminals trip over their own carelessness and hand up the evidence on a silver platter. But there was no Magnolia Rose listed in the catalog. I figured if Emmett had plans to sell the necklace, it would most likely be via some under-the-table scenario. I handed him back his catalog.

Meanwhile, Whit had been absently flipping through his copy of the auction catalog when he stopped on a certain page. "Huh. How about that? Lot 147: Marble bust of Queen Victoria, circa 1890. Consigned by E. Beauregard. I remember that bust. I was always enamored by it. Looks like Evelyn's selling it."

Emmett looked down at his wingtip shoes. "Whit, I know you and Tate were close once ... I'm sorry about what happened to him."

Emmett's eyes welled up, and he rubbed his nose with the back of his hand. For a murderer, he was a sensitive type, which strengthened my theory that it was a robbery gone wrong.

Whit patted Emmett's shoulder. "Thanks, buddy. It's still hard to believe he's gone."

Emmett offered a small nod.

I stood up. "Would you like to grab a cup of coffee with us?"

Emmett took out his phone again and looked at the screen. "Sure. I have a little time."

The three of us walked over to a refreshment booth and ordered some coffee. The coffee itself, a commercial blend that wouldn't win any awards but didn't insult my tastebuds, was a reliable but not remarkable brew.

I found a secluded area where we could have a quiet conversation.

The moment we sat down, I could no longer hold back. "Emmett, we need to ask you some questions about the night Tate was murdered."

His eyes opened even wider. "What? Why?"

"Parker's helping out the Beauregards with the investigation."

"I don't understand ..." Emmett looked as uncomfortable as a tax evader at an IRS convention.

"Jackson hired me to help find the murderer," I said. "I already talked to Annabelle, and she told me about your secret relationship. Your sister, Lila, confirmed it. In fact, she said you were madly in love with Annabelle."

Emmett bit his lip and gazed around the auction house as if looking for a quick getaway, but he wasn't going anywhere, because Whit and I had him cornered.

Emmett sighed. "Yes, it's true. She is the love of my life. What does that have to do with Tate's murder?"

I set down my cup of coffee. "We know Annabelle spends money like it grows on trees and that she's on a limited allowance and in quite a bit of debt. We also know you, the love of her life, would probably do anything for her, like steal a necklace and fence it."

Emmett shifted his gaze toward me. "What? That's ridiculous."

I continued sharing my theory. "Annabelle claimed you were supposed to meet her at the boathouse at six forty-five the night of the gala. I'm guessing you were supposed to have the necklace with you. I'm also guessing that you were a bit surprised to find Tate in the parlor during your heist. Was he already there or had he walked in on you?"

Emmett started twisting his narrow fingers in his lap. "No, he wasn't there ... I mean, I wasn't there! So, I don't know anything about that."

"It's okay, Emmett. You weren't expecting to find him there. It was an accident, a robbery gone wrong. Right?" I pressed.

Emmett gripped his cup and stared at me, his eyes

watering. He turned to Whit. "This is ludicrous. Whit, you know me. I'm not remotely capable of murder."

We sat in silence, the intensity of the moment blocking all external noise around us. I waited for the dam to break and the confession to start gushing out of Emmett's mouth.

"Look, Emmett, I've been doing this a while, and I know guilt when I see it. You'll feel better when you get it off your chest. We know it was an accident. We know you didn't mean to kill Tate."

Emmett's voice was a whisper. "I didn't kill Tate."

I studied his facial expressions, his eyes avoiding mine. He was hiding something. I could feel it in the space between us.

Whit patted my leg gently. "Parker ... maybe ..."

"No, Whit. He's hiding something."

Emmett lowered his head, his shoulders sagging with the weight of the accusation. His leg trembled so hard that the table vibrated slightly. I held Whit's hand and squeezed it. Wait ... just wait for it ...

Finally, Emmett sat up, his voice soft and resigned. "I was late because I was at Henderson's Hardware right before showing up at the Beauregard mansion. I needed to pick up some things to help Annabelle with her ... boat."

That wasn't exactly the confession I was banking on.

"Things? What things?" I was perplexed by his shoddy alibi.

He pulled out his phone and scrolled for a moment, then handed it to me, showing us an email of the receipt from the hardware store. "Here, look."

I took the phone, scrutinizing the receipt. The time

stamp showed six forty-two. There would be no way he could've made it to the house to murder Tate. I perused the list of items, which was long and mundane: duct tape, a wrench, and some cleaning supplies.

"Yup, there it is," I muttered, confirming his story. But as I scanned the receipt again, something caught my eye.

"A glass cutter?" I looked up at Emmett. "Why would you need a glass cutter for a boat?"

Emmett's face held a mixture of fear and regret. He folded and unfolded his arms at least three times and looked up and then back down at his cup. Then he finally spoke. "I ... I won't lie, I can't, I'm terrible at it. Obviously. Annabelle and I did have a plan to take the necklace."

Whit's hand tightened around mine as Emmett continued.

"I was already lollygagging and running late. I had reservations, you see. The moment I left Henderson's, I made up my mind I wasn't going to do it. Besides it was too late. And when I got to the gala, I was a mess and worried about telling Annabelle that I had chickened out. Then we heard what happened. It was awful that we were going to steal the necklace, but I swear to you, I didn't go anywhere near the parlor."

I handed Emmett back his phone. "Can you explain your text to Annabelle?"

"What text?" he asked.

I took out my phone and read the text. "Piece is listed. Hope we fetch a good price ... See you at the cabin."

Emmett cringed, then opened up the catalog and pointed to a diamond tennis bracelet. "That was for this piece of jewelry. When I told Annabelle I chickened out, she took off her bracelet and told me to auction it off. She's going to be upset. It didn't fetch what she thought it would."

A sour taste filled my mouth. My initial theory was partially correct but overall wrong. Emmett might've conspired to steal the Magnolia Rose, but he was not the killer.

CHAPTER 11

On our way back from Why, I slumped in the passenger seat, my earlier confidence deflated. Where did I go wrong? The puzzle pieces all seemed to fit, but they didn't make the picture I envisioned. "I can't believe I was so far off. I pride myself on being able to read the clues and people."

"Got to watch out for that pride. But hey, you weren't entirely off. You were right about Emmett hiding something. He was going to steal the Magnolia Rose necklace for Annabelle. Plus, he did end up auctioning off a piece of jewelry. Just not the Magnolia Rose. You just misread him as the murderer. It's hard to get a read on someone you've never met before. Don't be so hard on yourself, Parker."

My mind wandered back to the first time a similar incident occurred, which happened to be the beginning of my sleuthing career. Elementary school … The Case of the Missing Diorama.

"Missy Masterson's diorama ..." I said, without realizing that I was saying it aloud.

"Who?" Whit asked.

"My best friend from childhood. I was just remembering something that started my obsession with crime and solving it. You don't want to hear it."

"You know I want to hear it. Besides, we've got nothing but time."

"Okay," I took a deep breath. "For the science fair one year, Missy had poured her heart and soul into creating this incredible butterfly lifecycle diorama. I mean, it was a masterpiece, the kind of thing that made all the other kids' projects look like they'd been slapped together with glue sticks and a prayer.

"On the morning of the science fair, Missy and I practically skipped into school. She was so ready to show off her diorama to the world. But when we got to the classroom, the thing had vanished. Poof. Gone. As you can imagine, she was beside herself, and I, being the precocious little Nancy Drew that I was, decided to take matters into my own hands."

"I am certain you did."

"Yes. I questioned everyone, giving them my best 'don't mess with me' stare. I noticed Tommy Fincher, a boy in our class, acting shifty and suspicious. In my infinite nine-year-old wisdom, I decided he must be the culprit. I mean, he was always jealous of Missy's projects, so it made sense, right? I accused him on the spot, convinced I'd cracked the case wide open. But instead of admitting to stealing the diorama, when I pressed him on his whereabouts that morning, he broke down and confessed he was in the boys' bathroom, secretly trying to breed stink bugs in one of the stalls. This was confirmed when the custodian, Mr. Jankowski, was sent to investigate."

I side-eyed Whit.

His grin was about to explode into full laughter. "So Tommy was innocent of the diorama theft, but you knew he was guilty of something…"

"Yeah, but I wanted to find the thief…"

"You never found out?"

"Years later, when I was in high school, I was going through my old diaries, and I came across the pages from the time of the theft. I spotted something that clicked everything into place. In grade school, I had a crush on Max, Missy's year-older brother, so there were many entries about him at the time."

"Ah-ha! The plot thickens!"

"Yeah. So, I remembered that Max was the king of sibling pranks. I decided to call him up."

I went into podcast-narration mode. "So, I dialed his number, and my heart pounded with a mix of anticipation and grade-school nostalgia. When he answered, I didn't waste any time with small talk. 'Max, remember that time in elementary school when Missy's diorama went missing during the science fair?'

"There was a pause on the other end of the line. Max then said, 'Uh, yeah, I think so. That was ages ago. Why?'

"I took a deep breath. 'Because I think I know who took it. And I think it was you.'

"Another pause, longer this time. 'What makes you say that, Parker?'

"'I was going through my old diaries and found an entry from the day of the theft. I saw you coming from the boiler room area that morning. It was odd, but I didn't think much of it at the time because you and your buddies were always sneaking around forbidden areas of the school. But now, it all makes sense. You were the prank master, and hiding Missy's diorama would have been right up your alley.'

"Max let out a long sigh. 'Oh wow! You got me. I did take that thing. But it was just supposed to be a harmless prank, I swear! I did hide it in that basement boiler room, thinking I'd sneak it back into the classroom before the science fair started. But then I got caught up talking to my buddies and forgot all about it. By the time I remembered, the fair was over, and everyone was freaking out about the missing project. I went back to get it from the boiler room, but it was locked, and I couldn't get it. Next time I was able to sneak in there, which was maybe a week later, it was gone. I guess the maintenance staff must have found it during their rounds and thrown it out with the rest of the debris. I felt terrible, Parker. I never meant for it to go that far.' So, there you have it. The Case of the Missing Diorama, my first gig."

"Bravo!" Whit rapped on the steering wheel. "You solved the mystery."

"Took me a few years, but I finally got there … It had been a hard pill to swallow, realizing I'd jumped to conclusions and blamed the wrong person."

"That's okay. We all make mistakes. You can dust yourself off and start over. I have confidence in you."

"Thank you for saying that." Whit's enthusiasm and encouragement helped me feel a *little* better about my error in judgment.

Just as we were approaching the town limits, my phone rang. I glanced at the screen and saw Jackson Beauregard's name.

"Hello, Jackson."

"Parker, I need an update on the investigation." His voice was curt.

I hesitated for a moment. I didn't want to go into the business about Emmett. Something told me Jackson Beauregard favored positive news rather than dead-end leads. "I'm making progress. I've been following a few leads, but it's taking time."

"We don't have time, Parker." Jackson sounded a bit anxious, which was new for me to hear from someone who had exuded the confidence of a lion the last couple of times we spoke.

"Is there a specific reason for the sudden rush?"

"Something has come up, and now time is of the essence."

"Time is of the essence? What's that supposed to mean?"

"I've got a major business deal in the works, one that's crucial for the town's economy. If this murder isn't solved soon, the deal could fall through. Some of the whales are getting antsy and threatening to pull out."

"What kind of deal are we talking about?"

"It's a multi-use building development project that will bring jobs and revenue to Magnolia Grove. Lots."

I wondered if Jackson was more concerned about the potential loss to his pocket or finding justice for his brother's murder.

"I'll do what I can, but I'm sure you know the old saying … haste makes waste. Sometimes when things are rushed, important details are overlooked, and mistakes are made."

Jackson disregarded my comment and continued. "That along with another monkey wrench is causing me high levels of stress. I don't do well under stress."

"Um, okay. I understand, Jackson. If you don't mind me asking, what's the other monkey wrench?"

"A town hall meeting has been called to discuss the multi-use development details. Some issues have come up. A paperwork mishap. Nothing I can't handle. I just find it utterly amazing that *some* people in this town don't see the value in this sort of development …" Jackson's voice trailed off.

"You don't need to worry, Jackson. I'll do everything I can to speed things up. When is this town hall meeting?"

"Couple of days from now. Let's try to have this wrapped up by then," Jackson said.

I paused a moment and considered telling him about Annabelle and Emmett's failed plan to steal the necklace. But what would that buy me? Nothing. I decided to hold my cards close to my chest for the time being. I didn't want to stress Jackson out any more than he already sounded. "Will do."

"Good. And Parker, keep me posted." Jackson ended the call without any polite sendoff.

I put my phone down and stared ahead, the pressure mounting. I felt like what I imagined high-stakes poker players must experience when approaching the table before a championship. If I didn't get the case solved and soon, I'd be the town failure. I'd also be out of the second half of my payment and have to halt renovations on the cafe. But more importantly, the case would most likely go unsolved with Sheriff Sinclair leading the charge. And nothing ate at my conscience more than someone getting away with murder.

"That sounded important," Whit said.

"Not that important. Just the classic 'solve-the-case-soon-or-Magnolia-Grove-and-all-its-residents-perish' talk."

"What? That's crazy. Is he serious?"

"Jackson Beauregard doesn't seem like the practical joke type of guy. Yes, he is dead serious. Heavy investors are threatening to pull out because of the unsolved murder."

"Why would they care?"

"Imagine if you were big money and you poured your investment into a guy whose family might've had dealings with super-shady murderers. Or the guy you invested with turned out to be a murderer. Or his mom. Or his sister. They might find their entire investment gone. These big-money guys don't like that kind of potential risk. And now there's some town hall meeting in a couple days about the development. He sounds stressed."

I paused and jotted down some bullet points from my conversation with Jackson. The business deal hanging in the balance. The paperwork mishap. And of course, the accelerated timeline because of the town hall meeting.

Whit nudged me with his elbow. "Don't worry. You've got this. And I'm going to help however I can. We'll put our heads together and figure out the next steps. But first, I do need to get home and shower. I need a good night's sleep in my own bed. It's been a long couple of days."

I winked playfully at Whit, grateful to have him as a sidekick. "Sounds good. You can drop me off at my shop and take Clyde's car home. I'll get it later."

As we drove back into town, I recalled my reasons for moving to Magnolia Grove. I believed a simple place would eradicate crime from my life. I was starting to see the fault in my pie-in-the-sky thinking.

"You know, Whit, I gotta say, all this intrigue wasn't on the website for small-town living."

Whit chuckled. "On a positive note, you'll be able to add 'town savior' to your resume."

That one made me laugh out loud. I actually snorted.

When I put my notepad back into my bag, I saw the journal that Clyde had discovered. "Oh, before I forget ... Here's that journal I was telling you about. Lots of notes and riddles and numbers and poems. It's a *very* fascinating read."

"Great! Can't wait to check it out."

JUST BEFORE DUSK, I entered my soon-to-be neighborhood cafe, the familiar sounds of renovation filling the air. Clyde, now accompanied by three teenagers, worked tirelessly. Sawdust and drywall along with the aroma of pizza filled the space. After the whirlwind of the past forty-eight hours, this scene of normalcy was exactly what the doctor ordered.

Clyde greeted me with his usual warm smile. "Hey there, Parker. Got some new employees. Those there are my grandkids. Strong as oxen, all of 'em. Hey Colby, Blake, Franklin, come say hi to Miss Parker."

The teenagers shuffled over, offering shy nods that screamed, "I'd rather be anywhere but here."

I looked at each of them. "Nice to meet you, fellas."

"Yes, ma'am, nice to meet you, too." They all mumbled in unison.

Clyde clapped his hands. "Now, get back to work. I ain't paying you to stand around."

One of the boys, clearly the comedian of the group, piped up. "But Grandpa, you're not paying us at all."

"Heh. Don't get sassy, Colby, or else I'll have you scrubbin' the floorboards with a toothbrush."

They elbowed one another and laughed at some inside joke then went back to work.

"How did it go with Emmett?" Clyde asked.

"Not as planned. Turns out he didn't kill Tate, but he was hiding something. He and Annabelle were planning to steal the Magnolia Rose necklace."

Clyde stroked his puffy beard. "Well, ain't that something. So, what's the next move?"

"Not sure yet, but I'll figure it out. By the way, how's everything going here?"

"Smooth as Tupelo honey. We're making headway. Foundation finished up much faster than expected. Looks like our timeline shortened a bit. Nellie Pritchett stopped by too."

"What for?"

"Just nosing around. Scooping up information for that town hall meeting. Probably wants to report on your progress."

"I'll stop by and see her. I need to do some nosing around myself. I hit a dead end and need to figure out my next lead. Standing still won't get you anywhere."

"Ain't that the truth! Speaking of which, I best get back at it. Don't wanna be here too late."

I waved my goodbyes to the crew and turned to leave.

On the way out, I bumped into Clyde's friend, Dr. Rufus Delacroix. The retired professor of archeology smoothed his combover.

"Oh, pardon me, Parker. Didn't see you there!"

"Hi there, Rufus. What are you doing here? Came to see the colossal mess I got myself into?"

"Ha! I'm sure Clyde will get you fixed up in no time."

"Judging by the way things are going so far, I have complete confidence in Clyde. He's a miracle worker!"

"Yes, he is. He told me he uncovered the Elliots' hideaway for that old bootlegging racket. That kind of stuff piques my curiosity. Had to swing by to check it out. You know, those Elliots got into quite some trouble back in the day. They were a colorful bunch. They used secret tunnels under the town. And there might still be hidey-holes with valuables hidden away. If you can believe that."

He laughed and looked over my shoulder into the shop.

I thought about Penelope's journal. "Huh. Maybe that's what some of those journal entries were about. Secret locations."

Delacroix jerked his attention back to me. "Journal?"

"Yeah, part of Clyde's discovery. It was in the hidden area behind the wall."

Delacroix rubbed his chin. "You don't say ... You think I could get a gander at that?"

"Well, I just gave it to Whit Hawthorne, but maybe after he's finished."

"Yes, yes, please add me to the list of interested readers." He looked at his watch. "Oh, by the way, how's the murder investigation going? Any leads? What about the necklace? It's a shame that such a beauty is no longer in our midst."

"So ... you've clearly heard I'm helping with the case."

"Well, of course. News travels fast in Magnolia Grove."

"Yes, it does. I'm working some leads. I'd rather not comment on them right now, though."

He looked at his watch again. "That's great, Parker. Leads are good. Well, I just remembered, I have an appointment. I'll have to check out the Elliots' old hidey-hole later."

Delacroix rushed off.

I shook off the odd conversation with Dr. Rufus Delacroix and started my walk to the guesthouse to call it a day.

CHAPTER 12

The next morning, I woke up in the guesthouse to Major once again licking my face. Looked like this was going to be our new daily routine. And I loved it.

I rolled out of bed, and he jumped down to the floor and rolled on his back for his belly rub. After a few good scratches, I went to the kitchenette to brew a fresh pot of coffee to prepare for the day. I reached for my prized bag of Sumatran Tiger's Eye, a bold blend with notes of dark chocolate and spice that never failed to kickstart my mental gears. As the rich aroma filled the air, I could almost feel my synapses beginning to fire.

I tossed Major a treat. "Beautiful morning, eh, Major? Not too humid. But I'm sure that hot blanket will descend on us as the day goes on."

He looked up at me and barked. I broke another treat in half and tossed it to him.

While the coffee brewed, I grabbed my notepad and

paper from my bag to review my notes. I looked down at Major, who was already begging for the other half of the treat.

"I need to talk this out with someone, and you're the perfect candidate."

Major barked in agreement, his tail wagging. Then he jumped up on the chair across from me and sat down, his ears perked up.

I began tapping my pen against my notepad as I flipped through the pages of nearly indecipherable shorthand. "Okay ... let's play detective ..."

The bubbling sound of percolation and the delicious aroma saturated the studio.

"We have Annabelle and Emmett, star-crossed lovers who were going to pull a Bonnie and Clyde and chickened out last minute. Their alibis are pretty solid, and after meeting Emmett, he isn't the type who could pull off a murder without falling apart and confessing. Annabelle, while spoiled and extravagant, doesn't seem like the type who would kill her own brother. She'd be too grossed out about it afterward."

Major cocked his head.

"Next up, Tate. Why was he in the parlor in the first place? He owed money to people, and that gave him motive to steal the necklace. But if that's the case, someone beat him to the punch. And why would he have waited until the night of the gala to steal the necklace? It seems like he could've taken it at any point. Maybe Evelyn had it in a safe? I don't know ..."

Major let out a soft whine, either sensing my frustration or begging for another treat. I got up and poured myself a large mug of the steaming brew and handed Major another treat for being such a good listener.

"And speaking of Evelyn. Hmm. She's a tough nut to crack. What would she have to gain? And would she kill her youngest son over a necklace?"

Major let out a sneeze.

"I agree. Long shot ... Let's not overlook Dr. Rufus Delacroix, who I didn't have on the list until our encounter last night. Something is off about that overzealous retired archaeology professor. The way he checked his watch multiple times, then rushed off right after we talked about the murder. He had the same nervous tick at the gala. And I'm not sure I trust anyone who uses the term *hidey-hole*. What's his deal? Is he just a harmless, eccentric guy with a thing for the past and a fixation on the time?"

I finished off my coffee and stood up. Major jumped down and shadowed me into the kitchen, where I poured another cup and tossed him another treat.

"And Major, don't even get me started on Sheriff Sinclair. She's had it out for me since day one. Something's not quite sitting well with that one either."

I sipped my coffee and cradled the warm mug against my chest. I glanced down at Major, who stared up at me with attentive eyes.

"I know, buddy. It's a lot to take in. There's a piece to this puzzle that's just not fitting."

Major barked as if urging me to continue.

"Thank you for your encouragement ... Now we arrive at Lila Bennett. She claims to harbor no resentments toward the Beauregards, but I don't fully believe that. But she was sick on the night of the murder. And Sinclair had crossed Lila off the list of suspects because none of the guests interviewed saw Lila at any point that evening. Besides, she doesn't strike me as the stealthy assassin type. What do you think, Major?"

He yipped and tilted his little head again. I tossed him one last treat. I finished that round of coffee and poured another cup. I sat back down at the table and reorganized a stack of loose papers, placing the estimate for the cafe renovations at the top. This jarred my memory back to Maggie Thomas and the pile of past-due bills sitting on the counter in her boutique.

"Okay, Major, hear me out on this one ... Maggie Thomas, the owner of Boutique Chic. She's obviously well behind on her bills. We both know that financial stress is a great incentive."

My phone dinged. It was a text from Whit.

Parker—come by Miss Pattie's Breakfast Pantry. Interesting stuff in that journal you gave me. Also, I'll order for you. Pattie's Southern Sunrise or sweet potato pancakes?"

I texted back. *Yum! Sweet potato pancakes, please! Be there in five.*

He texted back with the smiley-face yummy emoji.

"Well, Major. You've been very helpful. It's time to eat and dig up some more clues."

Major wagged his tail.

Miss Pattie's Breakfast Pantry was a charming Southern restaurant situated on one of the small streets off Main. It had picnic tables out front with red-and-white-checkered cloths. Whit sat at one, flipping through the pages of the journal. The scent of fresh biscuits and sizzling bacon wafted in the air.

"Morning, Whit," I sat down opposite him.

He closed the journal and beamed at me. "Morning, Parker. Your pancakes are on the way."

"What'd you order?" I asked.

"Farmhouse steak and eggs with a side of hash browns."

"That sounds good!"

"It's better than good," he said.

"So, I had a productive morning reasoning things out with Major."

"Major? Clyde's dog?"

"He's a good sounding board."

"Ha! Did you two come up with any new leads?"

"A few. But the main one I want to pursue is Tate Beauregard."

Whit stopped sipping his coffee and set it down. "Tate?"

"Yes. I'm trying to figure out why he was in the parlor that night. My guess is to steal the necklace to pay off his debts."

Whit frowned. "You sure you want to go this route?"

"Hear me out … I'm just spitballing, but *maaaaybe* he and one of his 'associates' made an under-the-table deal.

Necklace in lieu of the debt stacked up against him? And something went wrong. Maybe this associate got greedy or panicky or was just your average psycho killer and things went downhill from there..."

"If that's the case, you're implicating two of the Beauregard siblings as thieves. Sure you don't want to throw Jackson in there for good measure? At this point, it might be easier to figure out which Beauregard didn't want to steal the thing."

"I don't have Jackson or Evelyn on the list ... yet. Either way, we need to pay the sheriff a visit and see if we can get Tate's phone records. We might need some of that southern charm of yours to butter up Sinclair."

"You remember she arrested me, right?"

"Exactly. We can use that to our advantage." I folded and unfolded my napkin.

The waitress, an older lady with short gray hair and a name tag that said Barbara Lynn, strolled over to our table and placed two steaming plates down on the red-and-white-checkered tablecloth.

"Morning. You must be the infamous Parker Hayes."

"I'm infamous now?"

Barbara Lynn winked and topped off Whit's coffee. "Anything else I can get you, sugar? Some coffee?"

"No thanks, I've already had three cups."

"Okay, then. You wave me down if y'all need something." She set the check down on the table.

Whit snatched the bill and stuffed it into his pocket. "Now, about this theory of yours ... First, you might want to slow down on the coffee. Second, seems a bit, I don't know, much."

"I don't think so. Annabelle was going to steal it."

Whit rubbed his chin and stared off for a moment. "Yeah, that's true. I just don't want to believe it."

"Yep. I know."

I poured a heap of syrup onto my sweet potato pancakes and cut into the stack. I took a bite and melted. The flavor and sweetness were overwhelming and perfect. "Oh, that's good."

Whit dug into his steak and eggs. "Miss Pattie knows her stuff."

"So, you mentioned you found something in the journal."

He pointed at the journal with his fork. "This thing is pretty much chock full of meticulous record keeping, clever riddles and old-timey prose. But there is one interesting mention about the Beauregards in a poem."

"A poem?" I took another bite of the pancakes and closed my eyes, wondering how anything could taste that good.

"I guess you could call it a poem ..." Whit flipped open the journal and turned to the page he had bookmarked and read, "In circles grand, where Beauregards hold sway, they yearn for MR. Rivière's presence day by day. Yet loyal he stands, with us through and through, his heart aligned with lineage true."

I took the journal and read the words to myself. "Well, well, Mr. Hawthorne. I didn't realize we were solving the mystery of 'The Bachelor: Early 20th Century Edition.' Sounds like this Rivière guy was quite the heartbreaker."

"Weird thing is, if he was such a player on the scene in the 1920s, I've never heard of him. Not that I know everything about everyone who ever lived in town, but I do know my fair share. I even looked into him this morning and couldn't find a thing."

I took another bite and savored it. "As fascinating as this is, I'm not sure how it helps us find a modern-day murderer or a missing necklace. Unless you think Mr. Rivière's ghost is floating around town, snatching jewelry and offing Beauregards?"

Whit looked a bit sheepish. "I don't know, I'm new to this detective stuff. Maybe the historian in me finds too many boring things fascinating."

I gave him an encouraging nod. "Hey, it's not bad to pull on threads that catch your eye. The trick is knowing which ones to follow and which ones lead to dead ends. We'll figure it out."

I handed the journal back to Whit. "For now, let's put a pin in the entry. I want to pursue the Tate-phone-record angle first before we go full *DaVinci Code* on this Rivière mystery."

Whit looked up from his steak and eggs and smiled as Lila Bennett strolled out of the restaurant with a to-go bag in her hand. She wore a black-and-white zebra-patterned kaftan that rippled in the breeze.

"Hi Lila," Whit called out.

"Oh, morning, you two." Lila's oversized black-framed glasses slipped down her nose.

"Picking up breakfast?" Whit asked.

"Yes …" Lila looked at me. "I'm so glad I ran into you. Parker, I apologize for my reaction to you suspecting my brother of stealing the necklace. Emmett told me everything. I'm mortified he would even entertain doing such a horrible thing. Of course, I'm sure it became clear to you that Annabelle was the mastermind behind the hijinks."

"No worries," I said. "Emmett's in the clear."

"Any other leads?" she asked.

"A few …"

She was about to say something when she spotted the journal sitting on the table. "My word. That looks just like some of the journals from my collection!"

"Clyde unearthed it in a secret chamber in my building. No bones with it, though." I laughed.

"May I?" She fumbled with her to-go bag for an awkward moment.

Whit took the bag and handed her the journal.

She flipped to the front and read the name. "My goodness. This is riveting! Penelope B. Elliot. Did you know this belonged to my great-great aunt?"

Whit wiped his mouth with his napkin. "I knew the 'B' stood for Bennett, but I was planning to verify the genealogy and who exactly Penelope was. Thanks for clearing that up!"

Lila's face brightened. "She and her twin sister Priscilla were devoted diarists. I have some of Priscilla's journals. The sisters were amazing at keeping records. They were adventurous, romantic and loved writing poetry …"

Whit perked up and took back the journal and flipped through the pages. "Really?"

Lila could barely contain her excitement. "Oh yes. They loved crafting coded messages and challenging each other to scavenger hunts in the tunnels under the town. Emmett and I used to try to find them, but many of the ones we found were either locked up or filled in. I tried explaining this to Dr. Delacroix, but that didn't stop his obsession with the tunnels."

"Dr. Rufus Delacroix?" I asked.

"Yes, he keeps asking if he can study Priscilla's journals. Silly old man. Retirement must be boring him to death. Do you think I could take this? It'd fit right in with my collection."

I looked at Whit, then to Lila. "Well, it's rightfully your property, but do you mind if we hold on to it a bit longer? I'm intrigued. I might discover some nuggets about the building I bought. You never know … Maybe I'll find a hidden tunnel or some moonshine! If I do, I'll go halves with you."

"That sounds like a plan!" Lila fumbled with her purse and found her keys. "Okay, I better be on my way. Good to see you both."

She turned to leave, then Whit held up her to-go bag. "Don't forget this."

"Oh my, yes. Thank you, Whit. I would forget my head if it weren't attached to my body now, wouldn't I!" She grabbed her bag.

"Before you leave," Whit said, "do you happen to know

the name Mr. Rivière? He's mentioned by Penelope in the journal."

"Really?" She paused a moment and stared off into the sky. "Mr. Rivière … Hmm … Can't say that I do."

"Okay, well, thought I'd ask. Have a good day."

"Yes, have a good one, Lila," I waved.

She waved back, turned and strolled off, her kaftan blowing like a sail.

CHAPTER 13

Fortified by Miss Pattie's hearty breakfast, Whit and I headed to the station. Our mission: to obtain Tate's phone records. As we approached, I steeled myself for another face-off with Sheriff Sinclair.

Leigh Ann Fletcher sat slouched at the front desk. Her fingers flew across her smartphone screen, her focus on her phone suggesting that solving the world's problems via text was far more pressing than attending to visitors.

"Good morning." I leaned up onto the front desk. "We'd like to see Sheriff Sinclair."

Leigh Ann didn't bother looking up from her screen. "Sheriff's busy."

Whit stepped next to me. "Leigh Ann. Come on, now. Just tell her it's important."

Leigh Ann huffed and pushed a button on the desk phone.

Whit and I strolled over to the waiting area in the lobby. The seating consisted of a few mismatched armchairs, a tattered couch with some hand-stitched cushions and an end table with a stack of outdated magazines. Across from the lounge area was a table with a coffee pot simmering under a bulletin board covered with community notices and a few missing pet posters. We strolled over that way.

"So, Whit, I'm intrigued by these tunnels I keep hearing about. First Delacroix, now Lila ..."

Whit straightened up; his deep brown eyes brightened as he cleared his throat. "Those tunnels have an interesting origin. During the Prohibition era, they were bootlegging tunnels. Here's where it gets fun. The Beauregards and the Bennetts became the preeminent Whiskey Barons of the region. The Beauregards excelled in manufacturing, while the Bennetts mastered distribution."

"Wait," I interjected, "I thought they hated each other?"

"Yeah. Ironic, huh? Despite their longstanding feud, their mutual hatred was matched only by their mutual dependence. Quite the paradox, wouldn't you agree?"

I grinned at his enthusiasm. "Fascinating."

Whit in full historian mode was a sight to behold. He picked up the coffee pot sitting on the side table, filled up a Styrofoam cup and handed it to me.

I took a sip of the lukewarm liquid that tasted half-burnt and bitter. "This town needs some real coffee," I choked.

"That's why you're here. Just drink it fast. It might taste awful, but it's fully loaded." Whit chugged back the despicable coffee.

I tried my best to take a few gulps, but it wasn't worth it. I tossed my half-full cup into the trash bin.

About fifteen more minutes slogged by until finally Sinclair came stalking down the hall toward us. Her hair was pulled back into a tight bun, not a strand out of place. She wore her standard-issue tan uniform shirt of the county sheriff's department, crisp and pressed as if it had just come off an ironing board. I wondered if she had a supply of them in her closet or if she dry-cleaned the same one at the end of each day.

"Morning, Whit," she said, then gave me a sharp nod. "Parker."

"We'd like to see Tate's phone records." I nervously tucked a strand of hair behind my ear.

She put her hands on her hips and frowned. "Why is that?"

"Because I'm investigating the murder."

"I thought by now you would've solved it since you're such an expert."

Ooooh. The sheriff knew how to grate my last nerve. I wanted to say something snarky back, but Whit instinctually took over the conversation.

"We just want to look into a hunch."

"A hunch, huh? You think that Tate maybe offed himself?" Sinclair chuckled at her dumb joke.

"Yeah, that's it..." I tried hard not to roll my eyes. "We'd just like to see those phone records from the day of the murder. Jackson is getting antsy about wrapping up the case."

"You going to pull the Jackson card every time you need something?"

"Yes. He's the ace in my pocket."

"Well, I can tell you right now who Tate called that day. One of them is standing right next to you." She glared at Whit, then continued, "He also contacted his local bookie, a known loan shark and his favorite pawnshop. All alibis check out. And trust me, these are the type of people that would've been noticed if they were anywhere near the gala."

"May I just see the records, Sheriff?" I asked.

"Come on, Amelia," Whit said, his hands spread wide in a pleading gesture. "We're old friends. I voted for you. And you did throw me in jail."

Sinclair cracked a slight grin. If there was such a thing as Amelia Sinclair loosening up, that was the closest I'd seen yet. She stalked off to her office and a few minutes later returned with a couple of pieces of paper.

"Here you go. But you're spinning your wheels. And don't leave the station with them. You can read them right here in the lobby. Leave them with Leigh Ann."

I took the folder. "By the way, Sheriff."

She raised her sharp brows and waited.

"Did you get the report back on what could've caused the blunt-force trauma?"

"I did."

"Did it say what it was?"

"It was something with a dull edge."

"Hmm. That *really* narrows it down."

"Just don't leave the station with those phone records." Sinclair pivoted and marched back to her office.

Whit and I sat down with the list of phone numbers. I took a snapshot. We handed the pages to Leigh Ann, who didn't acknowledge us, and we walked out.

We found a park bench in a shady spot and sat down.

I took out my phone and pulled up the photo of the records.

Whit pointed to one of the numbers. "That one's mine, so you can ignore it."

I started examining the other numbers, but ... "Whit."

"Yeah?"

"I can't ignore your number."

"Why not?"

"Because he called you five times that day!"

Whit was silent for a moment.

A heavy feeling settled on my chest. I didn't want Whit to be involved in this mess, but it was hard not to wonder. And if he was involved, I didn't want to be blinded by my ... well, you know.

He pressed his lips together and scratched the back of his neck, then sighed.

I asked, "Care to explain?"

A few more moments went by in slow motion. I knew Whit had been with me at the gala, so there's no way he could've committed the murder ... but could he have been involved in the planning? Or maybe he was the mastermind? Paranoia started creeping in.

"I'm telling you; it was nothing relevant to the case. Trust me."

I wanted to trust him, but since he'd been holding back on me, the water now seemed tainted. Doubt began to trickle through my veins like poison. Was I losing my touch when it came to reading people? Because so far, I seemed to be zero for two.

I exhaled and looked over at Whit. "Please just tell me. I want to trust you, but I won't if you don't tell me."

"Okay, it was over money. A lot of it."

"And you couldn't tell me that?"

"I didn't want you to think I had something to do with this whole thing."

"Well, now you're looking pretty suspect."

"Fine, Parker. He kept calling me and telling me that he was going to pay me back. But then he said he needed more money for just a few days. And that's when we got into the argument before the gala. I ended up telling him not to worry about paying me back and to get help for his gambling addiction. Then I told him to leave me alone and never contact me again. That argument was our last conversation. He was a friend of mine. And he died. And the last thing I told him was I never wanted to talk to him again."

Whit stood up and paced around the bench.

"You have to trust me, Parker. I have nothing to do with any of this. I'm just a historian who was trying to help out a friend who had a really bad gambling problem and wound up getting murdered. So, it's been a little hard for me to talk about."

I stood up and took Whit's arm. "Hey, I'm sorry. I didn't mean to press."

He pulled away. Tears streamed down his face. "Well, you did. Look, I need some space right now."

Whit walked away, leaving me alone in the park.

∽

CLOUDS LOOMED ON THE HORIZON. I sat on the park bench, my mind a battlefield of conflicting emotions. On one side, guilt gnawed at me for pushing Whit too hard; on the other, suspicion whispered that he was more involved than he let on. As I wrestled with this internal tug-of-war, my phone buzzed. Jackson Beauregard. Just what I needed.

"Parker, I need you in my office immediately," he said, his voice tight.

"Can it wait, Jackson? I'm kind of in the middle of something."

"No, it can't wait. Get here now."

I trudged over to Jackson's office, my mind still reeling from my conversation with Whit. When I walked into the office, I was greeted by Jackson's stern face and, to my dismay, Evelyn Beauregard sitting posture-perfect in a chair, her expression a mixture of anger and disdain. Of course, Sheriff Sinclair had notified Evelyn of my inquiries about her late son's phone records. Because, why not?

"Parker, have a seat," Jackson said, gesturing to the chair opposite his desk.

"What's this about?" I asked, already knowing I wouldn't like the answer.

"Can you give me an update on your investigation?" Jackson asked, leaning forward.

"I'm trying to find Tate's killer, Jackson. Same as always."

Evelyn glared my way. "I'll tell you about her investigation, Jackson. Miss Hayes wants to ensure each and every Beauregard is held in suspicion and our names dragged through the mud. What were you thinking, Jackson, in hiring this meddling little outsider."

If Evelyn's voice could've been measured by an emotional thermometer, it would've read *icy contempt.*

I held up my hand. "I'm only trying to find out who killed Tate. My investigation is about justice, not about dragging anyone's name through the mud."

Evelyn fixed her gaze on me, but her words, dripping with venom, were directed at Jackson.

"First, she accused my Annabelle—your sister—of murder, and now she's snooping around my deceased son's phone records like some common vulture. She's just taking your money and laughing all the way to the bank as she tries to bring us down, to destroy everything we've built. For all we know, she's an infiltrator hired by the Treadwells, the Bennetts, or even those backstabbing Sutherlands! How much more of our family's dirty laundry does she need to air before you see what's really going on here?"

I tried to keep my voice calm. "I'm following every lead, Evelyn. I'm getting paid to uncover the truth, even if it's uncomfortable."

Jackson, looking conflicted, tried to mediate. "Parker, I need to know if you're getting closer to a resolution. This needs to end soon. Before the town hall meeting."

"I'm close to solving it," I muttered with little to no confidence.

Evelyn chimed in. "Well, honey, you better wrap this up and stop trying to sabotage this family and its legacy. Who's your next suspect? *Me?*"

Before I could stop myself, the words tumbled out. "Well, Tate was known to keep some pretty questionable company."

I instantly regretted saying it. Evelyn's face contorted with rage, her cold resentment transforming into white-hot anger.

"How dare you!" she exploded. "You need to watch yourself, Miss Parker Hayes!"

Jackson, visibly torn, nodded reluctantly. "I'm sorry, Parker, but I have to agree with Evelyn on this. Please, just be careful with your words and accusations. That will be all for now."

I got up and left the office, feeling more dejected and isolated than ever.

The sky decided to join my pity party, unleashing a torrent of warm summer rain. Perfect timing. They say God has a sense of humor, but this felt less like a knee-slapper and more like a practical joke where I was the punchline. My mind was a whirlpool of doubt and confusion, threatening to drag me under. With each drop, the weight of the case pressed down harder, a reminder that my time—and my list of allies—was shrinking faster than my already dwindling self-confidence. Some out-of-retirement amateur sleuth I was turning out to be.

CHAPTER 14

*D*esperation breeds inspiration, or so they say. In my case, it led me straight to the town hall, domain of Nellie Pritchett, town clerk and self-appointed know-it-all. I sloshed through those doors like a sopping wet cat, my last scraps of investigative dignity hanging by a thread. If anyone could possibly assist in unraveling this mess of a case, it would be Nellie—whether she meant to or not.

The spacious reception area boasted polished wood floors and enough antique furniture to outfit a small museum. Finding the front desk deserted, I decided to explore. I walked down the hall, reading names on doors and wondering if the rainstorm had kept people tucked away in their homes, safe and dry.

At the corridor's end, I discovered Nellie's office nestled right next to Mayor Camden's.

"Knock, knock," I announced, poking my head into the gardenia-fragranced office.

"Parker Hayes! What a delightful surprise!" Nellie chirped, waving me in. "Oh dear, you're soaking wet!"

"Yes, I am. Just got dumped on."

"You know what they say about the weather here ... if you don't like it, wait twenty minutes and it'll change ..."

Nellie emerged from behind a desk that looked like a paper factory had exploded. Stacks of folders teetered precariously, peppered with empty mugs and assorted junk. The chaos seemed fitting for the human whirlwind that was Nellie Pritchett. "Please excuse the mess. It's been such a busy morning."

I bit back a smirk, suspecting Nellie's definition of "busy" involved more gossip-gathering than actual work. "I was hoping you had a few minutes to chat."

"Of course, dear! But first, let me offer you some of Miss Pattie's famous lavender shortbread cookies." Nellie produced a tin that had been resting on some papers on her desk. "You simply must sell some of her treats at your cafe when it opens."

I took a cookie and bit into it. The shortbread practically melted on my tongue; the subtle lavender flavor was perfectly balanced with buttery sweetness. It was, without exaggeration, the best cookie I'd ever tasted.

"Wow," I mumbled, still savoring the bite. "These are incredible. You're right, I definitely need to talk to Miss Pattie."

Nellie showed a look of joy, pleased with my reaction. "I told you!"

"I'm actually here to discuss other matters."

"Let me guess ... This is about the Tate Beauregard murder."

"Got it in one," I replied. "How'd you know?"

"Honey, if it's got a heartbeat in this town, my finger's on its pulse."

"Clearly," I said, taking another bite of the delicious cookie.

"Word is, Jackson Beauregard hired you as a private eye. Isn't that thrilling?" Nellie beamed like a proud parent. "I figured you wouldn't turn down any offers he made, especially with all those renovation costs piling up."

I sighed. "Initially, I took the job to prove Whit Hawthorne's innocence. Now I'm not even sure he's not involved somehow. And I doubt Jackson will pay me the other half, considering how spectacularly I'm failing to figure this out. The more pieces I get, the blurrier the picture becomes."

"Now, now, ease your mind and take a deep breath," Nellie soothed. "I'll give you a piece of the puzzle that's clear as day. Whit Hawthorne has nothing to do with any of this mess. He's about as straight as they come."

"I want to believe that. But right now, I just can't."

"Oh, honey, let me tell you something about Whit Hawthorne that'll set your mind at ease." Nellie leaned in. "A few years back, Whit inherited a small fortune from a distant relative. I'm talking serious money, the kind that turns heads in a town like this."

She paused for effect. "Well, you should've seen how fast the scavengers descended. Every shady businessman and get-rich-quick schemer in a fifty-mile radius was suddenly Whit's new best friend, pitching him 'can't-miss opportunities' left and right."

I raised an eyebrow. "And?"

"And you know what that boy did?" Nellie grinned with admiration in her voice. "He gave it all away. Every last penny. Donated the entire inheritance to the Pass It Along Widow and Orphan Foundation right here in town. Said he already had everything he needed and figured they could use it more than him. Now, does that sound like the kind of man who'd get mixed up in some shady plot to murder his friend? Whit Hawthorne's got a heart of gold and a moral compass that doesn't quit. If he's involved in this mess, I'll eat my hat—and I love all my hats."

"Thanks for that reassurance, Nellie. Hearing this sets my mind at ease. Anyway, I'm stuck, and since you seem to know everyone in town, I'm wondering if you have any insights."

"I'm happy to help with the case, but let's not talk here. Let's grab a cup of coffee."

I followed Nellie as she whisked down the hall to the kitchen, where she poured two cups of coffee and handed me one. I took a sip and had to stop myself from spitting it out.

"So, what do you think?" she asked, taking a sip.

"Hmm."

"Exactly. That's why we need an aficionado such as yourself. You can't find a decent cup of coffee within fifty miles of Magnolia Grove. I'll be sure we keep our shelves stocked with your blends. In fact, I'll tell all the establishments in town to buy bulk from you."

I laughed and set down the cup. "Sounds like a plan."

"Come on, let's go sit on the porch."

Outside, we nestled under the protection of the screened-in porch, listening to the rain tapping overhead. We looked out onto a beautiful courtyard surrounded by manicured bushes and a sprinkling of bird baths. At every turn, Magnolia Grove offered up picture-perfect backdrops.

Nellie slurped her coffee. "So ... what can I help with?"

"I'm looking into what I might've missed. Sinclair hasn't exactly been a team player."

Nellie shook her head. "That Amelia Sinclair can be a bit ... stubborn as a mule sometimes. I don't mean to be a gossip."

I found this statement ironic.

"I'm here because I'm just trying to figure something out, and you seem to be in the know ... Leading up to the gala, did you see or hear anything that seemed suspicious? Particularly concerning Tate."

"Tate was just Tate. Always happy-go-lucky. A bit foolish when it came to finances. Poor Evelyn helped him out as best she could. But he got in over his head and started 'borrowing' pieces of her jewelry and other such items and taking them down to that grimy ol' pawn shop. Personally, I think that's why she took out the extra insurance on the Magnolia Rose. Don't tell anyone you heard it from me."

"Wait a minute. Evelyn took out extra insurance on the necklace?"

Nellie lit up. "She sure did. I have copies of the notarized documents to prove it."

"Really?"

"Evelyn asked for my assistance in making a list of all the items that would be on display that night. She needed me to notarize the list against all the insurance policies on the items. Extra policy on the Rose. Very recent. I forgot to mention, I'm also a notary."

"Of course you are. So … did she have any specific concerns about Tate stealing the necklace?"

Nellie swiped the air with her hand. "No, no. Nothing like that. She kept going on and on about that necklace and strangers coming into her home to view the priceless heirloom. And how she wanted to be extra cautious because it'd be a shame if something happened to that necklace. After all, she may not seem it, but that Evelyn Beauregard is a somewhat paranoid woman. And you didn't hear it from me, but I have a feeling she's very concerned about finances. Especially with Jackson tying up much of the Beauregard money in this gamble of a project of his. Don't let her stoic demeanor fool you." Nellie finished the last of her coffee.

"And you didn't find it strange that the necklace just happened to get stolen?" I asked.

Nellie stood up and walked around the screened-in porch. "I did find it curious. But sometimes paranoia pays off. I think Evelyn Beauregard would go to any length to protect what belongs to her family. Or what she thinks belongs to the family."

I scribbled in my notebook. "What do you mean by *thinks belongs to the family?*"

"Oh, forgive me. I'm just carrying on now, aren't I? Well, the history of the Beauregards isn't exactly squeaky clean. I'm not saying that to be ugly. It's pretty well known that most of these powerful families don't get to where they are by the straight and narrow. Let's just be completely honest ... Take for example that old Bennett property that the Beauregards took over, quite possibly by what might be considered dubious means. Oh, I don't know, must've been fifty or sixty years back. And poor Maggie Thomas who still owns a small slice that cuts right into the property line. The very same property where they want to build that hideous new multi-use building. Now I'm not saying there's anything criminal going on, but the Beauregards have been known to utilize their influence to try to squeeze people out. And you didn't hear it from me, but Maggie's property taxes have gone up considerably, if you know what I mean ..."

My wheels were turning as Nellie rambled on. I thought back to Maggie's stack of past-due bills on the counter at her boutique. Wanting to protect her property and drive a dagger into the heart of the Beauregards would be cause for motive. Maggie Thomas was also the one who ran to Sheriff Sinclair and reported the heated argument she overheard between Whit and Tate before the gala. That was the reason the sheriff locked up Whit. Misdirection disguised as "assistance" is something I've seen suspects use many times over.

Nellie continued. "Anyway, I know that after the necklace was stolen, Jackson submitted the notarized list with the insurance claim."

I stood up. "Thank you, Nellie. I appreciate your help, but I better get going."

She sprung up. "I'm happy to be of assistance. Now, are you sure there's nothing else I can help with?"

"No, Nellie, you've been a tremendous help."

"Well, sweetie, that's just what I do. Now, you get on to finishing up those renovations so we can get some decent coffee in this here town of ours. And I'll see you at the town hall meeting. It should be an interesting one. Half the town is for the new building, the other half is against it."

"Oh, I wouldn't miss it for the world. I'll be sure to bring some popcorn."

The rain stopped pattering, and a break in the clouds overhead allowed some fresh rays of sunshine to beam through.

Things were looking up. Now I had another lead.

CHAPTER 15

The little bell above the door chimed when I entered Boutique Chic. The shop was empty save for Maggie, who was arranging a display near the front window. She turned at the sound of my entrance, and her glamorous face brightened.

"Parker! What a pleasant surprise. Come to add to your wardrobe?"

I shook my head, offering a small smile. "Not today, Maggie. I was hoping we could talk. I'm helping Jackson with Tate's murder case."

Her enthusiasm faltered slightly, but she quickly recovered. "Of course. Let me just finish this up."

I wandered around the shop, idly touching the soft fabrics of dresses and scarves while Maggie completed the finishing touches on the window display. Finally, she approached me, gesturing toward a pair of plush chairs near the fitting rooms.

"So, what can I do for you?" she asked as we sat down.

I decided to be direct. "Maggie, I've heard some things about your property and the Beauregards. I'm wondering if you could tell me more about that."

Maggie's cheerful demeanor slipped away, replaced by a guarded expression. "Oh, that little old business with the property taxes ... It's nothing."

"It doesn't seem like nothing. I've heard they've gone up astronomically."

Maggie sighed, her shoulders sagging. "You've been talking to Nellie, haven't you?" She shook her head. "That woman can't keep anything to herself."

"Is it true?" I asked.

"The Beauregards have been trying to buy me out for years. My little plot of land is smack dab in the middle of where they want to build their new development. When I wouldn't sell, well ... let's just say things got a bit more difficult around here."

"How so?"

"Oh, you know. Sudden increases in property taxes, mysterious issues with my permits, that sort of thing. Nothing outright illegal, mind you, but enough to make life ... challenging."

I leaned forward, my investigative instincts kicking in. "Maggie, I have to ask. Where were you when Tate was murdered?"

Her eyes rose with surprise. "You can't possibly think I had anything to do with Tate's death!"

"I'm just covering all my bases. Can you tell me where you were?"

Maggie's demeanor suddenly changed. She stiffened,

her gaze darting around the shop as if looking for eavesdroppers. "I ... I, uh, was around. You saw me there, remember?"

"Yes, I did. But you slipped away at some point, didn't you?"

Maggie twisted and clenched her fists on her lap. "Oh yeah, I had to go to the restroom, remember? We must've just not crossed paths again after that. It was quite a crowded affair."

"Maggie, I read through the witness statements, and you are notably absent at that point in the evening in all of them." I was bluffing. The witness statements all contained vague generalities, not particular absentees.

She bit her lip, clearly torn. Finally, she let out a long sigh. "Alright, alright. But you have to promise me this stays between us."

I leaned in closer, hoping to show her my trustworthiness.

Maggie lowered her voice to a whisper. "I ... I had a meeting. With Joseph."

"Joseph?" I repeated, confused for a moment before it clicked. "You mean Mayor Camden?"

A faint blush rose up her cheeks. "We've been ... seeing each other. In secret. His wife doesn't know, and with his position ... well, you could imagine the scandal if it got out."

I sat back, processing this new information. "So, you slipped away from the gala to meet with the mayor?"

"Yes," Maggie said, lowering her chin. "We met outside in the Beauregard garden hedge maze."

Of course, the Beauregards had a hedge maze.

"I see." My mind raced with the implications. "And how long were you gone from the gala?"

"I'm not sure exactly. We lost track of time. Then when we heard all the scuttlebutt, we slipped back in. I swear I had nothing to do with that awfulness and neither did Joe, I mean Mayor Camden."

I jotted down a few notes. "Thank you for being honest with me, Maggie. I know that wasn't easy."

As I stood to leave, Maggie caught my arm. "Parker, please. You promised this would stay between us. Joseph … the mayor … he can't know I told you. He could make things much, much worse with my property tax situation."

"I won't make this public, but I do need to confirm your alibi with the mayor."

"Please. You can't tell him!" She fumbled for her phone. "Look, I have a selfie of us to prove we were together during that time frame."

I examined the phone and verified the time stamp, then handed it back to Maggie. "Your secret's safe with me. But just so you know, secrets have a way of coming out in investigations like this. And secret liaisons with married politicians might not be a good idea. Even if you're trying to save your shop."

"I know, Parker. I know. I really hope you wrap things up soon," she said, absently adjusting her hair in the mirror. "And for the record, I have no intention of giving up my property. I might be willing to sneak in a canoodle here or there to try to save my shop, but I would never go as far as stealing a necklace and murdering anyone."

I left the shop. My mind was in overdrive. Maggie's alibi was solid, but it opened up a whole new can of worms. What else was the mayor of Magnolia Grove hiding? While none of this fit into the larger puzzle of Tate's murder and the missing necklace, I planned to keep my ear to the ground.

～

BEFORE HEADING to my next lead—Lucky Lou's Pawn and Loan—I needed to pay a visit to Whit. First, to retrieve Bertha the station wagon, and second (and more importantly), an apology was in order. I had come down hard on Whit earlier that morning, and after talking to Nellie, my confidence in him had been fully restored. I needed to make things right.

I walked up the steps to Whit's bungalow and knocked on the front door.

"Come in," he called out.

I entered the front office, which was much tidier than the last time I was here, and found Sheriff Sinclair rummaging around.

Whit peered up from his stack of papers and tried his best to force a polite smile.

"Parker," he said with a soft inflection.

I inched closer to his desk and cringed inwardly. "Hi there. How are you doing?"

"I'm alright. You?"

"I'm really sorry about earlier. It's just ... well, I don't know your history with Tate, and I'm a suspicious person by nature, as you've probably guessed."

Whit motioned for me to sit down in the armchair across from his desk.

"I get it, Parker. I'm sure seeing my number multiple times on Tate's phone records wasn't very reassuring. But you have to know I was neither involved with the theft nor the murder. I would've given the shirt off my back to Tate. I bailed him out *multiple* times over the years."

Whit swiveled around in his chair and faced one of the bookshelves behind his desk. The shelves were filled with old books and journals and leather-bound volumes about the history of North Carolina. I spotted an antique magnifying glass and a scale, along with a few vintage cameras and framed photographs from people over the decades as well as postcards of historic Magnolia Grove. He reached for a framed photograph and stared at it for a moment. "Strange to think this picture was taken at the spot where Tate died."

I reached out, and Whit handed me the framed photograph of him and Tate, just gangly teenagers, their arms around each other's shoulders. Tate had a mischievous grin while Whit smiled widely. There they were, in the parlor of the Beauregard mansion among the statues and family heirlooms and paintings.

"You guys look so happy."

"We were. Those were the good old days. Long before Tate's gambling addiction took off."

"I'm really sorry, Whit."

"I am too."

The space between us grew quiet. Just the sound of one of the antique clocks tick-tick-ticking. I wanted to run around to the other side of the desk and hug Whit. I had no doubt that he was innocent, not only because of what Nellie had shared with me, but also from Whit's body language and tone and the innocence he exuded. He wore a look of genuine sadness over the loss of his friend. A friend who he had tried to help many times only to lose in the end. From the night of the murder onward, Whit had been holding his grief at bay. Until I pushed him earlier and the dam had finally broken.

"I'm sorry I haven't been more sensitive. I was so focused on solving the case, and you were offering to help …"

Whit inhaled and gave a small grin, a real one, not a forced one. "It's understandable. Like you said, you didn't know the history between me and Tate. And I didn't show it because, well, we all deal with grief differently."

"You've got that right!" I said, really wanting to hug him. "So, do you think we can move forward?"

"Bygones," Whit said.

"Good." I handed him back the photograph. "So, I spoke with Nellie Pritchett earlier, and that led me to Maggie. Did you know that the Beauregards have been trying to squeeze her out of that property?"

"That sounds par for the course for the Beauregards. They do have a history of strong-arming anyone who has the audacity to be in their way … As far as Maggie's concerned, I knew she was in financial trouble. You think she was desperate enough to try to pull off stealing the Magnolia Rose?"

"Debt can make almost anyone desperate enough, but she has a pretty solid alibi. So, the next lead to follow is the pawn shop guy. If you're still interested in helping me, I'd love for you to come with me."

Whit stood up and smoothed down his shirt. "I'm one hundred percent in."

CHAPTER 16

Bertha the station wagon chugged along as I steered it toward the outskirts of town, where Lucky Lou's Pawn and Loan awaited. As we lumbered along, something nagged at the back of my mind, an itch I couldn't quite scratch. The feeling of wrongness clung to me like the musty smell that seemed permanently embedded in the car's upholstery. I knew if I let it simmer, like a good marinara sauce, the answer would eventually bubble to the surface.

Whit gestured toward a weathered sign reading "Lucky Lou's" hovering over a patch of dusty earth. I guided the station wagon into what passed for a parking lot, the suspension groaning in protest at the uneven terrain. We climbed out of the car, and the full glory of Lucky Lou's Pawn and Loan revealed itself. "Dingy" would have been a compliment. The gravel lot was bisected by a defunct railroad track. The building itself was a squat structure with crusty black bars on the windows. The neon sign above the door flickered and was missing a few letters, so it read: *ucky Lou's Paw and Lo n*. In the front window display sat a propped-up, tarnished tuba, an electric guitar with no strings and a mannequin wearing a wedding dress yellowed with age.

"Charming," I whispered.

"Don't judge a book by its cover. Lou might surprise you."

We walked under the tin awning sagging over the entrance and into the shop.

Inside, the place was a labyrinth of shelves stocked with everything from microphones to antique silverware.

A stocky man with a receding hairline and a permanent squint stood behind a display case counter at the back of the shop. I figured this was Lucky Lou himself.

"Afternoon," his baritone voice bellowed through the aisles.

"Hey, Lou," Whit called out as we headed to the back.

"Well, if it ain't the town historian. What brings you to my humble establishment?"

Pipe tobacco and stringent aftershave saturated the air around us.

"Lou, this is Parker Hayes. We're here to ask about Tate Beauregard."

Lou's eyes narrowed further, which I didn't think was possible. "What about him?"

I jumped in. "We understand Tate was a customer of yours. We're wondering when you last talked to him."

Lou squinted at me. "I've got a notion you already know the answer to that. What's your angle here, Miss Hayes?"

"No angle. I'm investigating Tate's murder at the request of Jackson Beauregard. And you're right, I do know the answer. You spoke to Tate the day he was murdered. In fact, you were one of the last people he spoke to."

Lou folded his arms across his sturdy chest. "So, you were testing me to see if I was gonna lie."

"I'm just gathering information. Did he ever mention anything about a necklace?"

Lou unfolded his arms and set his pudgy hands on top of the glass display case. He tapped his ringed fingers on the surface in a repetitive *click-clack-click-clack*. The fact that the display case housed numerous jagged-edged knives didn't help to ease my nerves. He drew in a deep, wheezy breath and exhaled slowly.

"I don't go yapping details about my clientele's private business matters. Especially when they …" A flicker of regret crossed over his ruddy face. "Well, you know …"

Whit eased in a little closer and patted Lou's arm. "It was a shock for all of us, Lou. We're just trying to get to the bottom of what happened."

Lou wiped a minuscule tear from his squinty eye. "Look, me and Tate go way back, and I don't like to speak ill of the dead."

"We're not here to tarnish Tate's memory," I said. "We're trying to figure out what happened. We want to find the killer and get justice for Tate."

Lou wheezed. "Alright, I'll tell you what I told that

stick-in-the-mud sheriff, but this stays inside these here walls. Got it?"

Whit and I nodded.

"Okay, then. Tate did mention a piece of jewelry. The day he went on to meet his maker, he'd called me and told me he'd be coming by with it in a couple days."

"Did he specify what type of jewelry?" I asked.

"Nope."

"Was this unusual for Tate? To pawn jewelry?"

"Nope."

"So, he'd brought in other pieces in the past?"

"He'd bring in lots of stuff. Coins. Jewelry. Electronics. Heck, I could keep going…"

"Were you at the gala the night Tate died?" I asked.

Lou let out a hearty laugh. "Do I seem like the gala type? I told that starch-collared sheriff I wasn't anywhere near that place."

"Where were you?" I asked.

He looked at Whit. "Your little friend here certainly dots her T's and crosses her I's … I was right here behind this counter. Old Man Murphy was unloading his entire record collection, and it took a good two hours to get her done. I have it all on tape." He pointed to the various cameras throughout the shop.

"Hmm. Okay. Well, appreciate your time." I shoved my notepad into my bag.

We were about to turn to leave the pawn shop with another unsuccessful lead when Lou spoke up.

"You know … here's the real corn in the cob. He didn't want to sell it."

I whipped around. "What?"

"Yeah, he wanted me to hold on to it for safekeeping until, as he put it, 'stuff blew over.' Said he'd reward me handsomely."

"Was this normal? Had he ever requested something like this before?" I asked.

"Tate? Pshaw. He was always starving for cash. That's why I found this request peculiar."

Whit asked, "You didn't ask him why?"

"Nah. When that much money's involved, I'm not the type to ask questions. After all, he is a Beauregard, and Beauregards do have money. I reckoned maybe that slick brother of his fronted him."

This piqued my interest. "What about Evelyn Beauregard?"

"His snooty mom? What about her?"

"You think she might've fronted him the money?" I asked. "Do you think she might've had an angle? In your professional opinion, of course."

He tapped the glass again. "In my professional opinion, that lady has more angles than a hexagon. But she made something clear to me on a recent occasion."

"What's that?" Whit asked.

Lou crossed his arms. "That if I had any further business dealings with her son whatsoever, she'd buy this here land, level my establishment and put a dump on top, which, as she said, I would be buried under. Those were her words."

"When was that?" I asked.

"I'd reckon about a month or two ago."

"But you still did business with Tate."

He smirked. "I did. I know that mama of his has some sharp claws, but Lucky Lou has tough skin and maybe not enough common sense to be afraid of the likes of her."

I took out my notepad and scribbled all this down. "Did you mention this to Sheriff Sinclair?"

"Most of it. The parts about the money and Tate wanting to pay *me*. And she told me not to tell anybody. But Miss Hayes, I actually like you. And I want justice for Tate, too."

I put my notepad back into my bag. "Thank you for your time, Lou. I'm sure you would've told us, but I have to ask. Has anyone come by looking to offload the Magnolia Rose necklace?"

Lou shook his head. "Nope. But if anyone does, I'll let you know."

∼

WHIT and I walked out of Lucky Lou's pawn shop and back to the station wagon. The pieces of the puzzle began to shift and realign in my mind. The loose threads that had been dangling in the wind were slowly weaving themselves into a pattern. It wasn't clear yet, but I could feel the familiar excitement building—the same sensation I used to get when working on a complex episode of my podcast. It was like watching a thousand-piece jigsaw puzzle come into focus.

I shifted the car into drive and eased out of the lot.

"Whit, I think I'm onto something here. Let me run this by you…"

"Lay it on me."

"When I went to talk to Nellie Pritchett, she mentioned that Evelyn had purchased extra insurance on the Magnolia Rose necklace. I think she hired Tate to steal it to collect money on the insurance claim. She probably promised him a big payment. And Annabelle mentioned that Evelyn had recently increased his inheritance. I'm thinking that during the feigned robbery, something went awry. Maybe things got heated because she found out Tate was planning to use Lucky Lou, a man she detested and had even threatened, to hold on to the necklace. She might've even gotten paranoid and thought Tate was going to go behind her back to sell it. Either way, things went sideways, and she accidentally killed her son."

"In my humble opinion, that's a pretty serious accusation, Parker. Insurance fraud. Murder."

"Nellie mentioned that Evelyn Beauregard was going on and on about protecting the necklace. In my experience with insurance fraud cases, perpetrators tend to overplay their worry to justify the need for extra insurance. In my episode 'Killer Premiums,' the wife had purchased extra life insurance on her husband, and in the months leading up to his death, she meticulously crafted an elaborate narrative about his deteriorating health. She frequently mentioned to friends and family how concerned she was about his sudden symptoms—chronic fatigue, dizziness and unexplained weight gain. To further bolster her story, she even scheduled numerous doctor's appointments, ensuring he was prescribed medications for fictitious conditions.

"Unbeknownst to her husband, she secretly replaced his medications with sugar pills and laced his food with a cocktail of drugs that simulated the symptoms of a severe heart condition. The pièce de résistance of her plan was a 'health tonic' she concocted, which was essentially a slow-acting poison that she claimed was an herbal remedy to help with his symptoms.

"The massive heart attack that ended his life seemed inevitable and tragic. She collected a cool million in insurance money without raising initial suspicions. However, her stepson, an amateur sleuth with a background in biochemistry, was suspicious of the rapid decline and pieced together her intricate web of deceit. His investigation uncovered the tampered medications and the toxic 'health tonic,' leading to her arrest and the forfeiture of the insurance payout."

Whit was quiet for a few moments, then let out a hearty sneeze and another.

"Bless you."

"That dusty pawn shop must've riled up my allergies. Anyway, we're going to need some solid evidence to back up your theory. Without the murder weapon, it's a little tricky."

The murder weapon. I'd been wondering about that missing piece of the puzzle for days. The only thing that the report stated was blunt force trauma, but nothing was found at the scene. So, it had to have been something portable that the murderer was able to leave with.

Then like a flash of lightning, the thought entered my mind.

"Whit, do you still have that auction catalog?"

"Yes, at my office."

"We need to grab it, then have Jackson meet us at the sheriff's station ... As much as it pains me to admit, I'd feel a lot more confident sharing the identity of the murderer in the presence of the local authority. Even if that local authority and I aren't exactly besties."

CHAPTER 17

Whit and I found ourselves once again entering the Magnolia Grove sheriff's station. Inside, the familiar scent of stale coffee along with Leigh Ann's usual indifference greeted us.

Jackson was already there, seated at one of the mismatched chairs in the waiting area, his face tight with the impatience of a busy man who didn't want to be pulled away from his work.

"Parker," Jackson said, then looked over at Whit. He stood up and stretched out his hand. "Whit."

Whit was about to shake Jackson's hand, then stopped. "No offense, but I either have allergies or a cold coming on. I'm sorry about your brother."

Jackson eased back a couple of feet. "Thanks. A real shame."

I told Jackson, "Whit's been helping me with the case."

Jackson took in what I'd just said, and his expressionless reaction made me think he found this bit of information curious then irrelevant. "Okay, you summoned me here to the station. Now what?"

I wiped my sweaty palms on my jeans and uneasily tucked my hair behind my ear. "Now we present all the information I've accumulated to Sheriff Sinclair, and hopefully she arrests the culprit of your brother's murder and we recover the necklace. Then you move ahead with your big business deal, I finish my cafe renovations, and the good townsfolk of Magnolia Grove get on with their lives."

"I like the sound of that." Jackson checked his watch, then turned toward the front desk. "Leigh Ann? Might you notify Sheriff Sinclair we are ready?"

Leigh Ann continued typing on her phone with the thumb of the hand she held it with and with her other hand hit a button on the desk phone. "Sheriff Sinclair? They're all here and ready to see you."

Sinclair's voice came through the speakerphone. "Send them in."

Leigh Ann clicked the button on the desk phone again. "Sheriff is ready for you."

Jackson, Whit and I made our way down the narrow hallway to Sinclair's office. Jackson knocked twice then pushed the door open.

Sheriff Sinclair sat behind her wooden desk, which was a bit more cluttered than before. She still hadn't unpacked the moving boxes. She looked up from her paperwork, her sharp eyes narrowing as she assessed us. Jackson pulled a chair out for me then took the only other one. Whit stood behind me.

Jackson crossed his legs. "How's little Sawyer doing?"

Sinclair exhaled. "Jackson, let's can the Southern gentleman pleasantries. I'm guessing you're here to discuss the case."

Jackson gestured toward me. "As you know, I hired Parker here to consult on this case to help expedite matters. And apparently, she thinks she has zeroed in on the culprit."

Sinclair scoffed. "Has she now?"

Jackson stared at me, waiting. "Well, Parker. Are you going to present your findings?"

I took in a deep breath, aware of the weight of what I was about to lay out on the table. "Jackson, before I begin, I want you to know this wasn't an easy conclusion to come to. What I'm about to share might be difficult to hear."

Jackson's piercing eyes studied me for a moment. "I'm a grown man, and I'm sure I can handle what you have to share. So, let's get on with it, Parker."

"Okay … I've been piecing together the evidence, and it's led me to a theory that involves your mother, Evelyn."

I paused for a moment to give them a second to swallow that bit of information.

Jackson's jaw clenched. "Go on," he said, his voice low and measured.

Whit gave me a reassuring pat on the shoulder.

I continued. "Based on the evidence I've gathered, I believe there was a plan involving the Magnolia Rose necklace. An insurance fraud scheme. But things didn't go as planned."

Sheriff Sinclair set her elbows on her desk and leaned in closer, raising one of her pointy brows.

"My investigation suggests that it was Evelyn who orchestrated this plan to have the Magnolia Rose necklace stolen and collect insurance on it. She enlisted Tate, promising him a share of the payout."

Sinclair smirked and leaned back in her chair.

I went on. "However, Tate decided to go off-script without involving Evelyn, and it was a decision that proved to be fatal. He chose to ask Lucky Lou to hold on to the necklace for safekeeping until the insurance money came in. Evelyn detests Lou and all he represents. After all, he's been Tate's go-to pawnbroker for the Beauregard family's heirlooms for years now. So, when she found out that Tate had involved someone she viewed as no better than pond scum, she when ballistic. She confronted her son at the gala while he was in the middle of the heist, and their argument escalated and turned into a physical altercation. I'm guessing in the heat of the moment, Evelyn hit Tate over the head with an object, causing him to lose his balance and fall against the bronze statue, which then toppled over. At that moment, their insurance fraud scheme turned into an accidental death. Evelyn, faced with the consequences of her actions, was forced to cover up not only the intended crime but also the unintended murder of her son."

As I finished up, I experienced an overwhelming feeling of satisfaction.

Sinclair chuckled to herself. "That's all very fascinating, Parker, but it's not plausible."

Of course, it was plausible. I had to guide Sinclair off her blind spot. "Sheriff, I completely understand that

Evelyn Beauregard has been an upstanding pillar in this community. But even wealthy people can do unbelievable things, especially in the heat of the moment. And allegedly she was very concerned over family finances." I removed the auction catalog from my bag and opened it to the page with the item Evelyn had put up for sale and pointed. "Right there. Lot 147. Bust of Queen Victoria, consigned by E. Beauregard. Just so happens to be immediately following the murder. It's the *only* thing she put up. Look, the perfect size ... and the dull-edged corners on the base. That is your murder weapon."

"That's enough, Parker." Jackson cut me off.

"Jackson, I understand this is difficult to hear. But please consider the facts. The extra insurance on the necklace. Your mother's hyper-concern over its safety that night. The extra inheritance and money promised to Tate. Financial worries. The sudden sale of the bust. Tate's request to pay Lucky Lou to hold the necklace, Evelyn's complete abhorrence of Lucky Lou ... I mean, she threatened him even. I'm not saying she's a cold-blooded killer ..."

Jackson shook his head and clenched his jaw. "You're way off base, Parker. My mother has always been overly cautious with protecting the Beauregard assets. Especially with regard to that necklace."

Sinclair rocked in her chair and grinned. "There's an actual reason why this little theory of yours isn't plausible."

I glared over at Sinclair, who seemed to be enjoying this interaction just a little too much. "What's that?" I asked.

Sinclair glanced over to Jackson, letting him explain.

"My mother has a rock-solid alibi for the time of Tate's murder."

"What do you mean?"

"She was with Dr. Delacroix," Jackson said.

My mind grasped for explanations, trying to connect the dots that seemed to be scattering every which way. Maybe I had it askew. Maybe Delacroix was the murderer ... Yes, it had to be Rufus Delacroix working with Evelyn. He was obsessed with the necklace. "That's right. She was with Delacroix. I saw them having a heated discussion ... They're in on it together. Maybe Delacroix is the one who killed Tate ..." I trailed off, realizing things were starting to sound a bit unraveled.

Sinclair held up a hand. "So now you're saying this was a murder for hire?"

I felt the ground shifting beneath my feet.

"No, but maybe he meddled and ..." I wiped the beads of sweat from my forehead.

Jackson cut in. "Let me just stop you there. My mother's alibi is also Delacroix's alibi. She had one of our security guards escort Delacroix off the premises because he wouldn't leave her alone about some cockamamie idea about some secret tunnel under our property. Everything's on video. The timestamp proves that neither of them were even close to the parlor at the time of death."

My heart was palpitating. "But what about the extra insurance your mother purchased? Don't you find that suspicious? It's enough to get a warrant to go inspect the bust she auctioned, right?"

"There will be no search warrant," Jackson said.

Desperate, I turned to Sinclair. "Don't you find any of this suspicious?"

"It seems like you're in over your head," Sinclair said with a smirk. This was the first time I'd seen actual contentment on the sheriff's face, and of course it was at my expense.

"Something isn't adding up," I said, rubbing my forearm.

Jackson's face was a thundercloud. "You know what's not adding up, Parker? You. Why didn't you come to me before having us come here? Clearly, I made a mistake putting my confidence in a *podcaster*."

The emphasis he put on the word "podcaster" took any last remnants of wind out of my sail. I opened my mouth to protest, but the cold look on Jackson's face told me it would be useless.

"And for that matter, you can consider yourself fired," he added.

Fired.

The word hit me like a battering ram to the gut.

Jackson stood up to leave. "Now if you'll excuse me, I've got business to attend to. Sheriff Sinclair, I'm sorry to have wasted your time. Good day, now."

And with that, Jackson Beauregard stalked out of the office, leaving a piercing silence in his wake.

I zoned out from the shock of my utter failure. Disappointment rose throughout my entire body. I found myself staring at the bulletin board behind Sinclair. Another one of her kid's crayon drawings had been pinned up. A small stick figure with curly brown hair wielded a sword and fought off a green monster. I could relate to that drawing, except in my version we would need a few more monsters.

"So, are you two ready to hang up your sleuthing hats now?" Sinclair's snide comment snapped me back into the room.

Whit patted my shoulder. "Parker, let's get going."

I stood up. "Uh, Sheriff, there is definitely something deeper going on with all this. And I'm going to figure it out —with or without your cooperation. I'm guessing it'll be without."

Sheriff Sinclair pointed her finger at my chest. "That's the first guess you got right."

Whit gave a curt nod, and we left.

Outside, the orange glow of the setting sun peeked from behind the trees. Crickets started their nightly chorus.

"Sorry that went down like that, Parker." Whit blew his nose.

"It's alright. I'll figure it out. Are you feeling okay?"

"Eh. I think I'm just worn out from all of this sleuthing."

I tossed Whit the keys to Bertha the station wagon. "You mind taking the car? I need some alone time to walk and clear my head."

"I bet. That was pretty rough in there. But I have to say, I'm still on your side, Parker. You'll be okay."

"I just know I'm not wrong. Okay, I might be a little wrong, but there's something … I'm missing."

"Don't be hard on yourself. You've single-handedly sniffed out at least three scandals happening in Magnolia Grove. You're not completely off base."

"Yeah, but I'm still short a murderer."

~

THE WALK back to Clyde's guesthouse seemed longer than usual, and Magnolia Grove's charm felt a bit more unsettling than quaint. I trudged down Main Street, my mind a tangle of theories and dead ends. The white clapboard church on the corner caught my eye, its simple steeple reaching toward the sky. A middle-aged man in khakis and a rolled-up blue button-down was carefully watering a bed of vibrant marigolds.

He looked up as I approached, his warm hazel eyes crinkling at the corners as he smiled. "Beautiful day, isn't it?"

I gave him an unconvincing, "Mmm hmm."

He briefly assessed me then set down his watering can and extended a hand. "I don't believe we've met. I'm Pastor Jasper Fry."

"Parker Hayes." I shook his slightly calloused hand. "I'm the new—"

"Ah, yes, the owner of our new neighborhood cafe!" His face lit up with recognition. "How's it going?"

I hesitated, then admitted, "Well, I've seen better days, to be honest."

Pastor Jasper gave me a sympathetic nod. "You know, I'm contractually obligated as a pastor to offer some words of encouragement here. Fair warning: mildly cliché metaphor incoming."

Despite my mood, I found myself chuckling. "Go for it, Pastor."

"My grammy Beatrice used to say tough times are like brewing coffee—it's a process of extraction, bringing out the hidden strengths we didn't know we had. And let me tell you, she made a mean cup."

His words stirred a memory. "Your grandma and mine would've gotten along. Mine had her own wisdom. 'Life's like a good cup of joe: it takes time to brew, love to perfect and patience to enjoy.' She never missed a Sunday service and always hummed hymns while she baked."

"Sounds like a wise lady." Pastor Jasper smiled, his soft drawl adding warmth to his words.

I felt a small curl tugging at my lips. "Thank you, Pastor. It was nice meeting you."

He turned back to his watering. "Hope to see you some Sunday, Miss Hayes. Our doors are always open."

"I appreciate the invite."

I continued on my way and felt a little lighter, the pastor's encouragement settling into my thoughts. I strolled by the Garden Inn and saw Nellie Pritchett sitting with two gray-haired women at one of the outdoor tables. They were sipping sweet tea and gossiping. I imagined within the next hour or so, I'd undoubtedly be the subject of their discussion. I could already hear the whispers ... "That city slicker Jackson hired to investigate his brother's murder just got fired. Accused Evelyn Beauregard! Can you believe it?! What a mess she made of everything."

"Parker!" Nellie called out to me, waving.

I ambled over to the table. "Hi, Nellie."

"This is the woman I was telling y'all about," Nellie said to her friends, gesturing at me. "She's going to solve the murder of Tate Beauregard." She then pointed to the women and spoke to me. "These here are the Ambling sisters, Beverly and Phyllis. They own the hair salon a few doors down from you. They've been there for how long now ... fifty years?"

The sisters mumbled in unison something to the effect of, "Yes, yes, I'd reckon so, you were just about knee-high to a grasshopper, Nellie, that's right."

I smiled at the endearing sisters. "Hello."

"So, how's the investigation?" Nellie asked.

I knew if I told Nellie what had just transpired, the news would be all over town in seconds rather than hours, so I just said, "I'm tying up some loose ends."

"Well, don't you worry your pretty little head too much. I'm sure you'll figure it out."

"I appreciate the encouragement. I better get going."

"You have a good night, Parker. And don't forget about the town hall meeting tomorrow afternoon. It's gonna be a good one. Allegedly there's a question about who owns the property where Jackson Beauregard wants to build that new multi-use building. Jackson himself came by earlier looking for old records, and we could not locate the original deed to save our lives. You didn't hear it from me though."

"Really? Who might be the original owner?" I asked.

Nellie shrugged. "Don't know. No original records ..."

For a speck on the map, Magnolia Grove was becoming a puzzle of mysteries.

"Well, enjoy your evening, ladies." I waved.

The Ambling sisters waved back, and the three ladies went back to their sweet tea and conversation.

∼

When I got to Clyde's, the sun had all but set, and dusk settled over the yard. Major greeted me at the back gate, jumping and scratching at my legs. His excited barks were a contrast to my pensive mood.

I entered the guesthouse and set my bag on the kitchen table and kicked off my sneakers. The ceiling fan whirred softly, its breeze carrying the aroma of toasted nuts and caramelized brown sugar from the pecan pie Clyde had left on the counter. There was no way I was going to bed without having a slice.

I cut into the pie, the knife sinking through the gooey filling and flakey crust with a satisfying crackle. The first bite was heaven. Sugary buttery nutty flavors filled my mouth and warmed my soul. Leave it to Clyde to know exactly what I'd need on a night like this.

"How's your day been, Major?" I said with a mouth full of syrupy pie.

He barked and stared at my plate. I grabbed a dog treat and tossed it to him.

"Well, I've had a *rough* day. No pun intended."

Major gobbled up his treat.

I took my last bite of the scrumptious pie, using every ounce of willpower not to get a second slice.

I collapsed onto the bed, sinking into the pillows.

Stretching out, I laced my fingers behind my head and gazed up at the spinning ceiling fan. Major, not one to be left out, hopped up and curled himself into a tight ball at my feet, his tail thumping softly against the quilt.

"I'm so close, Major. I've uncovered several guilty people, but not for the right crimes. And for the right crime, I can't find the guilty person. What am I missing?"

Major climbed onto my belly and cocked his head.

"And here I thought I had escaped all that." I scratched behind Major's ears. "Seems like most people in Magnolia Grove have something to hide. You're not a part of some underground crime syndicate, are you, boy?"

Major whined, his brown eyes looking up at me.

"Well, I'm stumped and my head hurts. What do you think I should do?"

Major hopped down and scratched at the throw blanket at the bottom of the bed. I dragged it closer to me, and he stepped on top of the blanket and began circling, digging and scratching at the material until he finally created the perfect nest for himself. With a contented sigh, he curled up into a tight ball, tucking his nose under the fabric.

"That's an excellent idea."

I turned off the lamp next to the bed and fell back against the pillows. I didn't even bother changing out of my clothes. It had been a long day. I was exhausted and very much in need of a good night's sleep. I hoped my subconscious would sort through all the details ricocheting around in my head and provide me with a clear answer in the morning.

Just when I was on the cusp of sleep, my phone buzzed. An unknown number.

"Hello?" I answered.

"Miss Hayes?" an animated voice responded. "Dr. Rufus Delacroix here. Sorry, were you sleeping?"

I yawned. "Just getting ready for bed. What can I do for you?"

His excitement was palpable through the phone. "Will you meet me at your shop tomorrow morning? I have something to show you that I found in the journal."

I sat up. "The journal?"

"Why yes, I went by Whit's earlier and after some persuasion, he let me borrow it. I promise you I'll return it intact. I must say, it's been a fascinating read. So, what do you say? Tomorrow morning?"

"Uh, can't you just tell me what you found?"

"No, ma'am. This must be seen in person."

"Okay ... Well, how does eight o'clock sound?"

"I was hoping earlier, but that works for me! Eight o'clock."

"Oh, and Rufus, just in case you hear any rumors ... I sort of accused you of being a part of a murder-for-hire plan. But obviously, I was wrong, and I apologize."

"Ha! Murder for hire, now that's a good one. No hard feelings. See you tomorrow!" He hung up.

As I set my phone down, I realized I was now wide awake. My mind spun like a kaleidoscope of possibilities. Major snored softly, already lost in his dreams. I envied him.

What could Delacroix possibly have to show me?

CHAPTER 18

After a night of restless tossing and turning, I awoke from my brief sleep to Major licking my face. I dragged myself out of bed. Major jumped down and trotted to the door. I let him out to do his business, then he scampered off to the main house, no doubt in search of his morning meal.

The promise of caffeine propelled me to the kitchen, where I fixed a fresh pot of my prized Cafe Luminoso—a fair trade, single-origin blend from the misty highlands of Peru. Its rich aroma filled the air as it brewed, already working its magic on my foggy brain.

I hopped into the shower, letting the warm water wash away the last traces of sleep.

Feeling somewhat human again, I dressed in a pair of well-worn jeans and a blouse. I returned to the kitchen, drawn by the fragrance of the freshly brewed coffee. I poured myself a cup and took a few sips, feeling the fog lift from my mind. My gaze fell on the leftover pecan pie.

Unable to resist, I cut myself a generous slice. The syrupy filling oozed onto the plate as I took a bite, savoring the rich, nutty flavor. It was a decadent breakfast, but hey, I figured I'd earned it after the few days I'd had.

Licking the last crumbs from my fingers, I texted Whit, asking him to meet me at my building. Dr. Rufus Delacroix had hinted at some important news, and I figured Whit would want to be in on it.

Caffeinated and sugar-boosted, I poured the remaining coffee into a thermos for Clyde, grabbed my bag and stepped out into the comfortable morning air, ready to face whatever the new day had in store for me.

I ARRIVED at my building a little before eight o'clock and was greeted by Clyde. The smell of lumber from the new framing filled the air with hope and possibilities.

"Morning, Parker!"

He stood next to a framed wall that hadn't been there the last time I was in the shop. He walked toward me, already sweating bullets.

"Wow, Clyde, I'm amazed at how quickly this is going." I handed him a thermos of fresh coffee. "Brought you some rocket fuel to help motivate you. Thanks for the pie. It hit the spot. I'm definitely placing some orders once this place is up and running!"

He opened the thermos. "Thanks, Parker. It's gonna be a long one. Lots of framing to finish up." He took a sip and whistled. "Goodness gracious, that is good stuff. A little extra incentive to hurry up and get your cafe finished.

We're all looking forward to some good coffee around here!"

"Well, Clyde, I have some bad news."

"What's that?"

"We need to put a pause on the renovations."

"Why's that?"

"Jackson fired me, so I won't be getting the second half of my payment."

Clyde frowned and rubbed his puffy white beard. "That's unfortunate. Why'd he fire you?"

"Long story short ... I made some pretty questionable assumptions based on some half-baked truths. I think by noon today half the town is going to drive me out on a rail, possibly after they throw tomatoes at me."

"Aww, Parker. Don't say that. I'm sure it's fixable."

"Well, you can't go accusing the town's most powerful matriarch of murdering her own son without some repercussions."

Clyde let out a long exhale and sipped some more coffee. "Well, about this here project ... we're still in the early stages, and the money you gave me is enough to get us to a good place until you figure out something."

I looked around at the framed walls and what looked to be the beginning stages of the new counter. We were so close to having the main portion of the cafe locked in that it'd be a shame to let it all go to waste. I thought about reaching out to my parents. As much as I didn't want to ask for help, I wasn't sure I had another choice.

Whit strolled into the shop followed closely by a lively Delacroix, who was carrying a pair of bolt cutters. I couldn't wait to get to the bottom of why the retired professor was carrying those. As they approached, one of the men, and I wasn't sure who, smelled like they'd been cooking some serious marinara sauce.

"Good morning, fellas," I said, nodding to them.

"It certainly is!" Delacroix said, his excitement palpable.

I looked at Whit. "Are you feeling any better?"

"A lot better. Thanks for asking." Whit scoped out the space. "Wow, Clyde, look at this place! You've accomplished quite a bit in a short amount of time."

Clyde laughed and smacked Whit's shoulder.

"I think we'll wrap up this project faster than butter melting on a hot biscuit. That's how much I'm looking forward to drinking down Parker's coffee on a daily basis."

Whit gazed over at me. "I haven't had any of the magical elixir yet …"

I felt a hint of a blush. "That's right! You haven't. I'll just have to brew you up some."

Delacroix was fidgeting and bouncing in place like a kid on Christmas morning. "That's great. Yes, yes. Coffee. Can't wait for the cafe to open. But I have news!"

We all stared at Delacroix.

"I found one!" he shouted.

"Found what?" Whit and I asked.

"An entrance to one of those tunnels that run under the city. And I didn't even need Miss Evelyn Beauregard's help. Not that she was offering it up, mind you. I figured it out on my lonesome! And it begins right here in your building, Parker! That's why I called you to meet me here."

He held up Penelope's journal.

"This here journal that Clyde so fortuitously found in the hidey-hole holds the key. Took a fair spell to put the puzzle pieces together, but it's all right there, plain as day! Land's sake, that reminds me, I best text Lila and let her know of my discovery! Naysayer that she was." He held out the bolt cutters to Whit. "Whit, can you hold these for me?"

Whit shrugged and took the bolt cutters. Delacroix fumbled with his fanny pack and took out his phone.

I whispered to Whit, "What do you think is happening here?"

"I don't know. Maybe he's completely lost his mind," Whit whispered back.

Delacroix put away his phone and cleared his throat. "If my theory is correct, this particular tunnel will unveil the bootlegging route, and if we're lucky, we might even come across some treasures! In case you were curious, that's what the bolt cutters are for. What do you say, Parker? Will you grant me permission?"

Delacroix's enthusiasm for the tunnels piqued my curiosity. Maybe an underground tunnel adventure was exactly what I needed to clear my head and get over the embarrassment of Jackson dismissing me from the murder investigation. Which I was still planning to figure out in case you were wondering.

"I'll give you permission on one condition," I said.

"What's that?"

"Whit and I come with you."

Delacroix waved a hand through the air and laughed. "Of course. Of course! I wouldn't have it any other way. Let's mosey!"

I turned to Clyde. "See you later. Wish us luck. Maybe I'll find some lost treasure to help pay off the rest of the renovations."

Clyde shook his head. "Heh. I reckon that would be something. Before you go into that tunnel, let's get you proper equipped ..." He walked over to his tool chest and grabbed a giant flashlight that had a shoulder strap.

I held up my cell phone. "Thanks, Clyde, but we've got light."

"Heh. Them cell phones ain't got nothing on this. They put out a dinky 40 lumens of light. This here is the RadiantMax 4000, and it's no joke. We're talking 120,000 lumens shooting over a thousand yards. It'll light up that tunnel like the sun at high noon in the desert. Y'all can never be too prepared."

Because he was so proud of the flashlight and made a good point, I took it from him. "Thanks, Clyde."

"Now here's the switch." He pointed at a button. "And be real mindful not to blast it into anyone's eyes, they'll be as blind as Saul of Tarsus for three days. I learned that one the hard way when I clicked it on the first time. I think I still see spots."

"Noted." I moved my thumb away from the switch and pointed the flashlight downward. "Dr. Delacroix, lead the way!"

Delacroix needed no time to respond to that request. He charged to the back of the building through the kitchen —which was coming along nicely, by the way—and opened a door that led into the boiler room. "Miss Parker, light, please!"

I flipped the switch. Even with the thing pointed at the ground, the room became considerably more visible.

"Clyde wasn't joking about that thing!" Whit said.

"There! Behind that old water heater!" Delacroix pointed into the room.

I aimed the light to where Delacroix was pointing. There was a half-door which looked like an entrance to a crawl space. We made our way to it, and Delacroix tried opening it. It didn't budge.

Whit moved close to the door. "Let me try. You mind if I kick it, Parker?"

"Go for it. But you'll have to buy me a new one if you break it. That one really ties the room together."

Whit gave the door a good heel-kick, then another, and the door burst open, an explosion of dust scattering through the air. As the dust settled, we peered into the pitch-black crawlspace. I swept the beam of Clyde's powerful flashlight into the area, revealing a world of cobwebs and forgotten items.

"Well, shall we?" Whit said, excitement now in his voice.

"Yeah!"

We crawled in one by one, Delacroix leading the way with surprising agility for a man his age. The musty space was cramped but not claustrophobic, and the three of us had to crawl because the ceiling was four feet from the floor. And I smelled it again—marinara sauce or something similar to it.

The beam of light revealed a hodgepodge of discarded treasures. A crate of empty bottles leaned against one wall.

"Look at this," Whit whispered, squatting down next to a stack of yellowed newspapers.

"And this!" Delacroix brushed cobwebs from a dusty painting propped against the wall. The portrait depicted a stern-looking man in Victorian-era clothing, his eyes seeming to follow us as we moved.

"Are we in the tunnel?" I asked.

"No, no, follow me," Delacroix said as he crawled ahead. Whit and I trailed behind him.

Delacroix abruptly stopped, causing Whit and me to nearly bump into him.

"What we seek is ... ah, here!" He ran his hands over some wooden floorboards, a look of intense concentration on his face. "I believe this is it! Please shine the light here!"

I directed the beam where he indicated, illuminating what appeared to be an ordinary section of flooring. But as Delacroix brushed away years of accumulated dust, I saw it —a faint outline of a trapdoor, barely discernible from the surrounding wood.

"The secret entrance," Delacroix breathed. "Help me lift it."

Whit moved forward, and together, he and Delacroix grasped the edges of the wooden panel. With a groan of protesting rusty hinges, they heaved it open, revealing a dark shaft descending into the earth.

A cool draft wafted up from the opening, carrying with it the scent of damp earth. As we peered down into the darkness, I felt excited and nervous.

"Well," I tried to keep my voice steady, "I guess this is where the real adventure begins. After all, nothing says 'fun morning out' like plunging into a dark, musty hole in the ground."

"Indeed, Miss Hayes. Indeed. Shall we proceed?"

"Ladies first." I slung the strap around my shoulder and allowed the flashlight to illuminate the black hole under me. I reached my foot down, felt a step of the ladder and tested it with part of my weight. It felt surprisingly stable for its age, so I put the rest of my body weight on it. On my descent, I cautiously tested each rung, and all of them turned out to be solid. Those rumrunners knew how to make a ladder!

"It's solid!" I called up. "About six feet."

Inside the tunnel, the stale dankness of old dirt hung in the chilled air. I aimed the flashlight beam ahead—the only directional option. On the dirt ground, there were two rudimentary tracks laid down. I figured that's how they moved the booze around town.

Down came Whit followed by Delacroix. As the older man's feet touched the ground, he let out a gasp of wonder. "Remarkable, simply remarkable. Ain't this just a sight to behold? We're standing where those clever bootleggers once trod, ferrying their illicit libations right under the noses of our law-abiding predecessors. This, my dear colleagues, is nothing short of history breathing before our very eyes!"

"Bullseye, Dr. Delacroix." Whit's enthusiasm boiled over. "It's one thing to read about these tunnels in old records, but to stand here ... well, it certainly puts things in perspective."

"Well, gentlemen, as exciting as it is to stand in this

damp, dark piece of history, I suggest we start moving before we become part of it."

"Alright, let's press on," Whit said, gesturing ahead.

The tunnel was wide enough for all three of us to walk side by side.

As we forged ahead, Delacroix's enthusiastic commentary punctuated our journey. Despite Delacroix's running narrative, I found myself distracted. Amidst the dank air, I kept catching those whiffs of what reminded me of marinara sauce. The smell tugged at my memory, but I couldn't quite place it. It was familiar, like pasta night at Enrigo's back in the city, but out of place in this underground tunnel. I focused on navigating the uneven ground, puzzled by the out-of-place scent. Delacroix launched into another historical tangent about Prohibition-era engineering, and I filed away the odd smell for later consideration.

A few minutes into our trek, the beam of my flashlight caught something on the side of the tunnel. A metal door, its surface mottled with rust, stood out against the earthen walls.

Delacroix and his combover leaped with excitement. "A door! Let's see what lies beyond it!" His gaze fell on the thick, rusty lock securing the handle. "Quick! The bolt cutters!"

Whit stepped forward, positioning the bolt cutters around the lock. He squeezed with all his might, but the ancient lock refused to yield.

"Parker," he grunted, "I could use some help here."

I handed the flashlight to Delacroix then moved to Whit's side and added my strength to his. Together, we bore down on the bolt cutters. For a moment, nothing happened. Then, with a sudden snap, the lock broke in two, clattering to the ground.

Delacroix rushed forward, yanking on the handle. The door groaned in protest but finally swung open, revealing … a solid brick wall.

I sighed. "Well, that's anticlimactic."

But Delacroix's enthusiasm was undimmed. "It's just one door of many, my friends. I'm sure a lot of them have been sealed off over the years. Who knows why they bothered with a lock. Onward! Our great discovery awaits!" He handed the flashlight back to me.

His determination was infectious, and despite the setback, we pressed on, deeper into the tunnel's belly.

We came across another door which was also sealed off. No lock to cut through this time.

We continued for another minute, then we came upon another tunnel entrance to the left.

Delacroix was beside himself. "I reckon that one leads under downtown if my sense of direction is still worth a hill of beans!"

I pointed the flashlight down the tunnel, and it looked the same as the one we were in.

"Which way?" I asked.

"Parker, point the light back up this way." Whit motioned toward the tunnel we were in.

I pointed the light ahead in the direction he requested.

"Way up there. What is that?" Whit asked.

"Let's find out!" Delacroix said, already making his way.

We walked about a thousand yards before coming upon an old sturdy wooden chest pressed against the wall.

"Treasure!" Delacroix sounded like a seven-year-old at this point.

He lifted the lid, and it squealed open.

And...

Empty.

All three of us sighed simultaneously.

As I scanned the immediate area around the chest, I noted an old rusty broken lock lying in the dirt. "I think someone has beat us to the booty. Well, this is turning out to be a bit disappointing."

Delacroix, undeterred, said, "Onward!"

As we pressed on, the tunnel gradually inclined. Suddenly, we found ourselves at the end of the road, facing another door.

"End of the line," Delacroix said, brushing the door as though it were a relic.

Whit took hold of the steel handle. "It's open!"

I moved closer, shining the flashlight on the thick wooden door. The old wood had been scarred by time but still looked sturdy. My foot kicked something that clanked. I pointed the light to the ground to find a broken lock.

"Look at this—the lock's been cut. Someone's been here already."

Whit pointed to the ground. "Are those footprints?"

The three of us examined the dirt more closely.

"They sure are," I said, noting these were made by more modern footwear due to the enhanced details of the prints.

Delacroix clapped his hands. "Let's go through and see what awaits us on the other side!"

The heavy oak door creaked open with a weary moan. We stepped into what appeared to be a hidden passageway within a house. The air here was different, less musty and damp. The walls were a mix of exposed brick and aged plaster. Old hooks hung on the walls where lanterns might've hung.

Whit scanned the area, his excitement increasing. "This is the Beauregard's place! These are the passageways I was telling you about, Parker. From when Tate and I were kids. I don't recall a door to any underground tunnels, though."

When we all filed into the narrow passage, I turned around to examine the door we had just come through. Once closed, it looked like a part of the plaster wall. No telltale sign that it was a door.

"Remarkable craftsmanship," Delacroix said, running his finger along the nearly invisible door edge.

We walked single-file through the narrow passage. There it was again: the overwhelming scent of ... marinara sauce or maybe pizza, and it was certainly coming from Whit.

"Whit, I hate to ask you this right now, but what on earth is that smell on you?"

"What smell?"

"Strong marinara sauce."

"Oh, it's probably the cold remedy concoction of Lila's. Essential oils of lemon, ginger and oregano. I had some left over from the last time I was sick, so I took it last night and again this morning. Works like a charm. But the oregano packs a potent punch."

"Hmm … that's curious."

Whit pointed to the end of the passageway. "Oh, whoa … look! That door … I'm almost positive it opens to the parlor."

Delacroix was surprisingly silent.

I rushed over to the door, turned the knob and swung it open. And we emerged into …

The scene of Tate's murder—the Beauregard's parlor.

My gaze swept across the opulent parlor, taking in the surroundings. The black-and-white-checkered floor, the art collection, historical artifacts, ceramics and statues—it was all as I remembered. Except this time as I gazed at the bronze statue of the Roman gladiator, a nagging sense of wrongness tugged at my mind. Memories started flashing before me … The crayon drawing of the stick figure fighting off the monster in Sinclair's office. The photo of Whit and Tate as teenagers standing next to the statue.

"The sword," I breathed. "It's missing from the statue."

And then it hit me. The smell on Whit. It was the same overpowering oregano scent I'd noticed the night of the murder. All the pieces fell into place.

"I know exactly what happened—" I began, but was cut off by a sharp, angry voice.

"What on earth do you think you're doing in my home?"

We whirled around to find none other than Evelyn Beauregard standing in the doorway wearing a plush pink bathrobe, her face a mask of fury and indignation.

Evelyn's eyes blazed as she pointed an accusing finger at me. "You! You've wasted my son's time and money with your ridiculous smear campaign. I'm going to have you arrested for trespassing!"

She then turned to Delacroix, her voice bristling with contempt. "And you, Dr. Delacroix. I've had quite enough of your nonsense. I'm going to have you committed to a shabby retirement home a few counties away where you can babble on about your tunnels and treasures to your heart's content!"

Finally, her gaze landed on Whit. "And Whit, I expected better from you. You're just a fool to be running around with these hooligans. What would your mother say?"

Evelyn began patting the pocket of her bathrobe, growing increasingly agitated. "I'm calling the sheriff right now and having you all thrown in jail!"

Realizing she didn't have her phone, Evelyn let out an exasperated growl. "I'm going to find my phone, and when I return, you better be gone or so help me …"

She stormed out of the room, her slippers clacking on the hardwood floor.

Delacroix, seemingly oblivious to the gravity of the situation, hurried after her. "But Mrs. Beauregard, if you'd just listen! The historical significance of these tunnels is immeasurable! We could be sitting on a goldmine of prohibition-era artifacts!"

Whit, looking torn, glanced at me before following them. "Mrs. Beauregard, please wait! I think Parker's just solved the case. If you'd just give us a chance to explain …"

Their voices faded as they disappeared down the hallway, leaving me alone in the parlor. I stared at the bronze statue of the Roman gladiator.

A soft click came from behind me. A cold chill shot up my spine.

Slowly, I turned to see Lila Bennett emerging from the secret passage, clutching an antique pistol. Her usual eclectic style was on full display—a flowing kaftan of geometric patterns. A collection of mismatched bangles jingled on her wrist as she held the gun, the sound strangely cheerful in the tense atmosphere. Her signature oversized glasses were askew and her salt-and-pepper pixie cut unkempt, as if she'd been running her hands through her hair in agitation.

"I'm sorry it's come to this, Parker," Lila said, her voice trembling. "But I can't let you ruin everything now. Not when I'm so close."

"Lila, you don't have to do this," I tried to keep my voice calm. "Whatever happened, we can figure it out together."

She shook her head, a nervous laugh escaping her lips. "You don't understand. I've waited years for this. The Beauregards have taken everything from my family. This was our chance to reclaim what's rightfully ours."

"The necklace? Is that what this is all about?"

"It's so much more than just a necklace. It's our legacy, our birthright. And Tate ... he was going to ruin everything."

As she spoke, I reached for the RadiantMax 4000 hanging at my side. Lila, caught up in her confession, didn't notice.

"I'm sorry, Parker. I truly am. But I can't let you leave this room knowing what you know."

Lila's face then hardened with resolve. As she trained the pistol on me, I acted on instinct. I whipped up the RadiantMax 4000 and flicked it on, aiming directly at Lila's eyes. The sudden, intense beam caught her off guard. She cried out, stumbling backward into the gladiator statue, hitting her head. She crumpled to the ground, unconscious.

I looked down at Lila's body, feeling a blend of relief and sadness. Footsteps approached the parlor, and I steadied myself for what would come next.

CHAPTER 19

Lila Bennett began to fumble around on the floor, rubbing the back of her head with one hand and patting her face to adjust her glasses with the other. I kicked the antique gun away, and it hit a nearby wall. I almost felt sorry for Lila, but she was going to kill me to keep me from exposing her secret. She was the one who had murdered Tate Beauregard the night of the gala. It all clicked into place when Whit mentioned Lila's herbal home remedy. I suddenly recalled where I had smelled it before--in this very parlor on the night of Tate's death. The overpowering scent of oregano was unmistakable.

"Hold it right there." Sinclair's voice jolted through the room.

I lifted my hands in surrender, just in case Sinclair got trigger-happy, and slowly turned around to face the sheriff, a deputy and Evelyn. Whit and Delacroix stood a few feet behind. Sinclair noted Lila's pistol on the floor and motioned for her deputy to secure it.

"Sinclair, I found your killer," I announced.

Sinclair let out a laugh. "Is that right? Now you're accusing sweet Lila Bennett?"

Evelyn shook her head in disgust. "This outsider has been a real nuisance. First, she accuses my daughter, then Emmett, then me and now Lila. You are unbelievable, Miss Hayes."

Lila mumbled and sat herself up. "What happened? Oh, my word. What's going on?"

I gazed down at Lila. "You hit your head, but you're okay. Probably a minor concussion."

Evelyn Beauregard fumed. "Will you tell me what in the devil is going on here?"

Lila was in tears. "Delacroix contacted me to tell me about the tunnels, so I decided to come and look. I brought my old pistol because, well, you never know what's down there … Then I heard voices and wound up in here, and that's when she blinded me with that flashlight!"

"Nice try, Lila," I said, shaking my head. "Sheriff, I'll explain everything if we all can just calm down."

Whit stepped between Evelyn and the sheriff. "Yes, just hear her out."

Delacroix added, "I'm dying to hear what this little lady has deduced!"

Sinclair looked at Evelyn and shrugged.

Evelyn waved her hand in the air and huffed. "Fine, whatever. But you're wasting your time."

Sinclair lowered her gun and moved deeper into the parlor toward me. The others followed behind.

"Do you mind if I get something out of my bag?" I asked the sheriff.

Sinclair raised her palm at me. "How about you slide the bag toward me, and I'll get it for you."

I did as she said, then instructed her, "In there is a catalog from the antique auction that took place in Why last weekend. Take it out and flip to the middle or so."

"Not the catalog again," Sinclair said in her spare-me-Parker tone I'd already come to know.

"Just trust me."

I waited as the sheriff dug around in my bag, taking out items and dropping them onto the floor ... my notepad and pens, a black scrunchie, some mints, my wallet, my phone, and finally she pulled out the catalog. Sinclair began thumbing through the pages. Whit inched his way over, peering over her shoulder.

"Look for lot #73," I said.

"There it is!" Whit pointed at one of the pages and read, "Lot 73. Late 19th century antique decorative sword with bronze hilt and intricate floral motifs, recently restored, provenance unknown. Anonymous seller. I knew I recognized that piece!" He looked up at me and beamed.

Evelyn moved closer in and scrutinized the photo, then looked over at me and gazed at the bronze statue of the Roman gladiator that Lila had just hit her head on. The same statue was toppled over during the robbery of the necklace and murder of Tate Beauregard. Evelyn looked back at the photo. "How did I not see that?"

Sinclair stewed over the photo. "See what?"

"The missing murder weapon." I did my best not to gloat as I said the words.

"Parker Hayes has just solved the case of the Magnolia Rose," Whit announced.

I squared my shoulders and addressed the group. "It was Lila Bennett in the parlor with the bronze sword. Lila used the sword to hit Tate over the head the night of the murder. She then took the necklace and the sword and escaped through the passageway over there. If you go about halfway down the passage, there's a hidden door that leads to an underground tunnel system. It was a system the Bennetts used for their bootlegging operation back in the day. One of the tunnels goes to my building. And I'm quite certain that another one we passed leads to the Bennetts' antique shop."

Sinclair let out a long sigh. "Why on earth would Lila Bennett want to steal the Magnolia Rose necklace?"

I turned toward Lila. "Because it belongs to the Bennetts."

Evelyn rested her hands on her hips. "It most certainly does not!"

I continued sharing my conclusion. "In the journal Clyde found hidden in the wall of my building, a journal which belonged to Penelope Bennett Elliot, she wrote about the MR Rivière. At first, I thought it was a person, but MR didn't stand for Mister Rivière. It stands for Magnolia Rose. I remembered the meaning of the word rivière from my podcast episode about the murdered jeweler, 'The 24-Karat Kill.' One of the victim's colleagues loved using Old French. Rivière is a stream of gems on a necklace—like a river—with one large central stone. Penelope was writing about the necklace."

Evelyn gasped and glared at Sinclair. "You're not falling for this malarkey, are you?"

"When the Beauregards announced they were hosting a gala and putting the Magnolia Rose on display, Lila Bennett saw her opportunity to get back what rightfully belonged to the Bennetts. Lila has known about the secret tunnels since childhood. That's how she got in and out of the parlor the night of the gala."

I paused a moment as everyone watched and waited.

"When Lila went to steal the necklace, Tate was already there for ... well, for reasons I've already stated. But Lila wasn't about to lose her one chance of getting back the necklace. There was an altercation between Lila and Tate, which led to the statue toppling over and Lila grabbing the sword to hit Tate over the head. To get rid of the murder weapon, she auctioned it off 'anonymously,' though I am sure if you further investigate, you will see that Lila's account has received the exact amount the sword was sold for, minus auction fees, of course. And if my suspicions are correct, I'm guessing you'll find the Magnolia Rose in a lock box in the Bennett cabin located in Why."

Just then, Lila Bennett rolled herself upright and stumbled toward us.

"That's right ... I'm going to reclaim all the property that is rightfully ours. I have recently found the original deed to the property the Beauregards stole from my family decades ago. The one that Jackson wants to demolish for his hideous new building. For generations these scoundrels have been bullying us Bennetts, robbing and stealing from us. I'm going to restore the Bennetts' name to its former glory, and the Beauregards' name will be left rotting in the sewer where it belongs. But I'm babbling now, aren't I?"

Sinclair walked over to Lila. "So, you're confessing to the murder of Tate Beauregard?"

Lila's gaze fell to the floor. "I didn't mean to kill him," she said, her voice cracking. "I just wanted the rivière. Tate wasn't supposed to be here."

Sinclair motioned for Lila to get up. "I'm sorry, Lila, but I'm arresting you for the murder of Tate Beauregard…"

Evelyn shot mind-arrows at Lila. "And the robbery of my precious Magnolia Rose necklace!"

"And that too." Sinclair turned Lila around and slipped on a pair of handcuffs.

"Well, I'll be!" Delacroix said.

Whit helped me gather up my personal belongings and put them back into my bag.

Sinclair glanced over at me. "Parker. I'll need you to come to the station for a statement."

"Of course, Sheriff."

Sinclair, her deputy and a tearful Lila exited the parlor with Evelyn in their wake.

"When I can expect retrieval of my property, Amelia?" Evelyn asked.

"When I get to it, Evelyn," Sinclair replied.

Their voices trailed down the hallway.

Whit put his arm around my shoulder, still smelling of oregano. "Proud of you, Parker."

"Thanks. But you helped tremendously. That oregano oozing off of you cinched the deal."

"Happy to oblige," he said, squeezing me.

Whit, Delacroix and I left the parlor—the non-tunnel route. As we exited the mansion, we passed Evelyn. She avoided eye contact with me. Not a word of gratitude over solving the murder of her son. I suspected she was more concerned about the fate of her precious necklace and whether or not she would be charged with potential insurance fraud. I had a sneaking suspicion she would skirt any consequences.

"That was the most thrilling ride I've had in a while," Delacroix said, rubbing his hands together.

"Well, thanks, Dr. Delacroix. You were a big help by locating the tunnel," I said.

"You're most welcome."

"Now what?" Whit asked me.

"I suppose before we head to the station, we get over to that town hall meeting and inform Nellie Pritchett that Lila allegedly found the original deed to the property and they might need to pause on the vote. Jackson's not going to be too happy about this."

"But you solved the murder," Whit said, lightly punching my shoulder.

"Yes, we solved the murder," I said, returning the favor with a light counterpunch of my own.

CHAPTER 20

The crisp morning air in Magnolia Grove carried the pleasant aroma of pumpkin spice and cinnamon. Autumn rustled in the breeze as I strolled through the heart of the charming storybook town. Shop owners unlocked their front doors and flipped over their open signs, waving to one another with that small-town enthusiasm that felt a bit less alien to me.

I gazed upon the historical building I had purchased, now transformed into my cafe, and felt a mix of pride and disbelief. Above the awning and glistening windows hung a wooden sign that read *Catch You Latte*. I'd thought the name was clever when I came up with it, but now I wondered if I'd be cringing at my pun for years to come.

Nah, I would always love it.

I felt a warm glow of satisfaction. This was my very own neighborhood cafe where I would soon be serving the town of Magnolia Grove specialized coffees and homemade and local desserts.

Clyde Honeycutt, my miracle-working handyman, stood outside with his dog, Major. How he'd transformed this dilapidated building so quickly was beyond me. I was half-convinced he could turn water into wood stain if the renovation called for it. His catchphrase "it's fixable" had proven to be less empty reassurance and more like a promise capable of moving mountains, or at least relocating a few load-bearing walls.

"Morning, Clyde," I bent down to pet Major. "And good morning to you too, fur-ball."

Major let out a bark that I chose to interpret as, "Congratulations on not completely screwing this up."

Clyde, looking dapper in khakis and a collared shirt, greeted me with a bear hug.

"Good morning, Parker!"

We stepped back, taking in the building's cleaned-up facade.

"A picture of beauty," I said.

Clyde whistled in agreement. "She sure is.

I unlocked the front door, and we stepped inside. Though I still needed to purchase furniture and decorate, the interior was stunning. The walls were painted a soft white, and some areas had exposed brick. The high ceilings with the exposed pipes had been painted black. Vintage-inspired light fixtures crafted from metal hung throughout the shop in lovely dome-shaped silhouettes. But the highlight was the enormous handcrafted oak counter and wooden stools at the far end of the shop. Behind the counter, speckled antique mirrored glass filled the back wall and gave the place a sophisticated vibe. The chrome espresso machine gleamed, a modern contrast to the cafe's vintage charm. It looked ready to caffeinate an army. My cafe was the perfect mix of past and present, with a shot of attitude.

"It's perfect, Clyde. Absolutely perfect."

"Not too shabby, if I do say so myself. So, Parker, beyond furnishing the place, what's next on your agenda?"

I scanned the empty space, mentally populating it with mismatched tables, chairs, and eclectic art pieces. The realization that the cafe was actually finished and almost ready for customers felt surreal.

Heading behind the counter, I announced, "Well, first thing's first. I'm making you a fresh cup of coffee. Your first free cup of a lifetime supply!"

I reached for a silver canister containing my prized Volcán Dorado, a rare blend grown on the mineral-rich slopes of an active volcano in Guatemala. The smoky, dark-chocolatey and earthy aroma of the freshly ground beans tickled my nose. I grabbed a French press from one of the open shelves and turned on the espresso machine for hot water.

As the machine warmed up, I reflected on the whirlwind since moving to Magnolia Grove. From my naïve first steps into this once-dilapidated building to Clyde's unwavering assurance that it was all fixable, the journey had been nothing short of incredible. I mused, recalling Nellie Pritchett's not-so-subtle push to attend the Beauregard gala, Maggie Thomas's kindness in outfitting me for the event, my first encounter with the eccentric Dr. Rufus

Delacroix, and that initial spark-filled conversation with Whit Hawthorne.

Then there was Jackson Beauregard, whose exorbitantly generous payment for the murder investigation of his brother helped finance the speedy completion of the café renovations. I was grateful he had given me the second half of the payment, and then some. After all, I did solve the murder. And I recovered the Magnolia Rose necklace. I think he also felt bad that I almost got killed. But who knows with a guy like Jackson?

I thought about poor Lila Bennett, who had traded her wardrobe of kaftans for prison-orange jumpsuits. She had been charged with second-degree murder and theft. To pay for a decent lawyer, Emmett Bennett ended up working out a deal with Jackson Beauregard, selling him the property that Lila discovered had rightfully belonged to the Bennetts. In the end, Jackson Beauregard got what he wanted and closed the deal for the multi-use building development, with the stipulation that Maggie Thomas would have a brand-new retail shop rent-free for the rest of her life. Sheriff Sinclair, not one to leave loose ends, ordered all access points to the old tunnels sealed off—save for one by the old courthouse, now marked with a stern "Authorized Personnel Only" sign. Dr. Delacroix talked his way into becoming one of those authorized personnel and immediately went on an exploration and excavation bender. We wondered if he would ever return to the surface.

As for Evelyn Beauregard, she not only got back her precious Magnolia Rose necklace but also managed to slither out of any legal entanglements. Her fancy, top-notch lawyer swatted away any attempts to use that old journal to question her ownership of the necklace. And insurance fraud charges? Please. They disappeared faster than a politician's promise after election day.

You bet I was convinced she was guilty. But according to Sheriff Sinclair—who clearly graduated from the "See No Evil, Hear No Evil" school of law enforcement—Evelyn was simply a victim of theft, and poor Tate was just in the wrong place at the wrong time. Case closed, tied up with a neat little bow, and swept under the rug. Because that's how justice works in Magnolia Grove.

I poured Clyde the inaugural cup, sliding the mug across the gleaming oak counter.

"Enjoy!"

Clyde took a sip and whistled. "Now *that* is a cup of coffee. Magnolia Grove won't know what hit it."

"Knock knock … You open for business?" Whit called out from the entrance.

I waved. "Whit! Perfect timing. Fresh cup coming up!"

Whit strolled up to the counter and greeted me with a peck on the cheek. "Congratulations, Parker. And Clyde, you outdid yourself. In my humble opinion, it's beautiful. Good morning, Major."

I poured Whit a cup and handed it to him. He parked himself next to Clyde on one of the wooden stools.

A few moments later, Nellie Pritchett whisked into the cafe.

"Good morning! And congratulations to you, Miss Parker Hayes. The place looks fabulous! Now how about pouring me a cup of that there fancy coffee? After all, I did rush those permits through for you." She winked.

Nellie saddled up next to Whit. I set down a steaming cup in front of her. Nellie snatched it up and took a sip and let out a glorious sigh. "Now, I suppose this is what coffee is supposed to taste like." She took another sip. "Yes, indeed, Parker. You're going to do just fine!"

As Nellie savored her first cup with a contented smile, I poured myself a cup and leaned against the counter, taking in the scene. These faces, once strangers, now were family.

I raised my mug.

"A toast to the future and the adventures that lie ahead!"

We all toasted and sipped our coffees.

Just as I set my mug on the counter, my phone vibrated. I noted the area code; it was from my old neck of the woods.

"Hello?" I answered.

"Parker Hayes. Long time. We need to talk." I recognized the familiar voice from my podcasting days.

"Oh yeah?" I tried to sound composed.

"I'll be in town soon. I'll swing by your cafe."

He hung up.

"Who was that?" Whit asked.

I plastered on my best "everything is fine" face, but I knew that if *he* was coming to town, trouble wasn't far behind.

Thank you for taking the time to read my book! There are millions of choices out there, so I appreciate you taking a chance on mine. Reviews are incredibly important because they help readers discover new books. If you enjoyed this book, please consider leaving a review—just a line or two would mean a lot to me!

To continue sleuthing with Parker Hayes, check out the next installments on Amazon: <u>Cafe Crimes Cozy Mystery Series</u>. If they aren't available yet, they will be soon!

If you haven't already, you can get my FREE ebook, A Sip of Suspense, about Parker's mysterious bus ride from the big city to Magnolia Grove when you subscribe to my newsletter: <u>Simone Stier Newsletter</u> or visit <u>simonestier.com</u>. By subscribing, you'll be the first to hear about new releases, cover reveals, special deals and giveaways!

My acknowledgments could fill a book. First, I'd like to thank my friend and savior, Jesus, for the gift of writing and for holding my hand through every storm. I'd also like to thank my amazing husband, Peter, for being the most wonderful writing partner and best friend. And many thanks to my family and friends for supporting my writing journey ever since I was knee-high to a grasshopper. And once again I'd like to thank you for reading my book!

<u>Cafe Crimes Cozy Mystery Series</u>
<u>A Shot of Scandal</u>
<u>A Drizzle of Danger</u>

[A Blend of Betrayal](#)
[A Measure of Mayhem](#)
[A Sprinkle of Secrets](#)
A Hint of Homicide
And more to come ...

Let's stay connected!
[Simone Stier's Amazon Author Page](#)
[Simone Stier's Facebook Group](#)

Simone Stier is a cozy mystery author who weaves tales of small-town intrigue, filled with charming settings and characters that feel like lifelong friends. Her stories draw inspiration from the quaint town in North Carolina where she resides with her husband and beloved dog. A passionate storyteller since middle school, Simone honed her craft by studying creative writing at the University of Maryland. A USA Today best-seller, she has shared her novels with readers around the globe. When she's not plotting her next whodunit, Simone leads Celebrate Recovery, binge-watches HGTV and dreams up delightful new cozy adventures.

Made in United States
Orlando, FL
27 February 2025